TREASURE OF THE AMERICAN DRAGON

The Wilder Chronicles

Jon Shannon

North Star Publishing

For Lori.

Thank you for three decades of love, support,
and encouragement.

CONTENTS

"Always remember, it's simply not an adventure worth telling if there aren't any dragons."
Sarah Ban Breathnach, Simple Abundance: A Daybook of Comfort and Joy

Chapter One

Walking the Dragon

My name is Wilder Blackwood. I like walking through the darkest parts of town. I prefer streets and sidewalks that don't have streetlights. It's the best way to avoid being seen. No shadows, only darkness. The weight of that darkness is like a heavy, comforting blanket. The stillness and calmness allow me to catch up on my thoughts. The murkiness of the night and the blackness of my companion's thoughts sometimes both intrude upon my own. My presence is the only thing preventing my sidekick's total random destruction and killing spree in the dim neighborhoods we walk through in the middle of the night. It's something that needs to be done. Otherwise, I can't imagine the horror. These houses and apartment buildings would be burnt to the ground, and my four-legged compadre wouldn't even blink an eye. He would look at me and say, "Oops, sorry."

To any nosy Nancy peeking out from behind their curtains into the street, they see me passing by their house in the semi-obscurity of the night with a dog by my side. Usually, that is a perfectly ordinary scene in any small town late at night. That's the difference between perception and reality, between what people think they see and what is actually there. Bocephus is no ordinary dog or even a dog at all. He is a dragon, like in an ancient myth or a fantasy movie. A dragon with a big, scaly, reddish body, a long neck, two flappy leathery wings, a long tail, and two flaring nostrils oozing tendrils of smoke. A classic-looking dragon, the kind of creature you'd see in Game of Thrones or How to Train Your Dragon.

I don't know where he came from or why a dragon presents as a dog, but it's true. I prefer walking him on the streets with the fewest lights because, for whatever bizarre magical reason, the shadows show his actual form. A shadow that is fierce and frightening enough to make a grown man wet his pants and heart skip a beat. Imagine a simple little French Bulldog casting a shadow the size of a garbage truck that looks like a winged dragon covered in scales with a long snout filled with razor-sharp teeth strong enough to rip through steel, snapping at the air for no reason other than to look frightening.

Bocephus realizes precisely what he is, but he lets me take him for walks regardless of that fact. He knows there's always a reward before the night is over, and we return to my little apartment above the sandwich shop off Main Street. Let's just say this isn't a good neighborhood to have a cat get lost. If it happens on a Tuesday, Thursday, or Sunday, you probably won't find the cat in the morning. However, Monday, Wednesday, Friday, and Saturday are safe days to lose a pet. We only walk three nights a week when I get off the dinner shift at work, which is enough for Bocephus. He's content to be a menace lurking in the dark, on the lookout for a midnight snack. People are perfectly safe, at least I think so. Time will tell.

We walk through the shadowless night, listening to the sounds of the city around us under the glow of the stars. It's late and most people are asleep, but there are occasional sounds of doors slamming a little too hard and a few TVs that need their volume turned down substantially. This time of night, the only people awake are the ones who have no business being awake. The ones who don't know how to be quiet for the sake of their neighbors. The people across the street don't need to hear what you're watching. Nobody is trying to solve the Jeopardy puzzle by listening to your television from a block away.

How did I end up in this situation, taking a dragon dog for long walks under the cover of darkness? I'll explain a little about magic, the world I live in, and the small role I play in it. As far as I can figure, the inherent laws of the universe require someone of the magical sort to have a sidekick. A familiar, most people call it. I am a practitioner of magic. I don't mean the kind of magician who does birthday parties or stage shows. No tricks or sleight-of-hand, I do actual magic. A magician in the real sense of the word, someone who works in the ether between this world and the next to bend the fabric of reality just enough to make sure things don't get too cock-eyed. Nothing as powerful or magnificent as a wizard, like in the movies and legends. I'm a few steps below that, for sure.

To an untrained observer, I may seem like an average New England millennial wearing jeans, a flannel shirt, and Timberlands. Still, I've saved countless lives in my map-dot hometown, operating in my own particular way. A slight motion of my hand or a muttered phrase under my breath is all it usually takes to make a difference in someone's life or prevent a disaster from taking place. Sometimes, it's covertly flicking a downed electrical wire away from where it might put someone in imminent danger or helping a car come to a stop in icy conditions before it slides into an intersection and saving a pedestrian from certain death. My magic is small but mighty. I use it with a purpose. A little magic push here and there, unnoticed by the people around me. I operate in the background, trying to keep people safe and prevent life in our little town from going off the rails.

Despite that, magic isn't something you can always control; it often takes on a life of its own. I was going about my days working at the restaurant, keeping under the radar and using my magic when people seemed to need the help. I was alone, gliding solo through a magical universe. This dog was unexpectedly plopped into the middle of my coastal Maine neighborhood. It just happened to be in my town, on the street where I live. Or maybe it was no accident at all. Perhaps it's the universe making sure a proper balance is kept. I was out for a late evening walk when I first encountered this drooling, gassy little mess. Somehow, it was attracted to me, and not in a way as if I seemed like a tasty morsel. Like a witch and her black cat, we bonded together. If I had known beforehand, I would've bought stock in the Twinkies company. I'll explain that part, too.

CHAPTER TWO

HOW IT ALL BEGAN

You could argue it was an accident or coincidence, but I would never believe it. Whether the dog found me or I found him isn't relevant anymore. The streets were empty on that early summer night, the air was still, and the stars were out in full force. The moon shone so brightly that the lunar beacon almost lit even the darkest side streets. Somehow, Bocephus appeared out of nowhere, like a moth drawn to a flame. I seemed to be that flame.

That first night, Bocephus followed me back to my apartment while I walked home from the grocery store a few blocks away. I live above a little sandwich shop, but my door is street-level with a narrow flight of stairs up to the third floor. The sky was clear and resplendent with stars, thanks to the lack of light pollution. This town shuts down around 8 pm every night, and there aren't many people or cars on the street. I had two bags of groceries, one in each hand. I like the reusable shopping bags with handles. They are much easier to carry, and I save a nickel every time because our state makes a store charge five cents for a bag. Call me frugal, call me an environmentalist, and I don't care. As I set the totes down on the sidewalk to fish my key out of my pocket, I felt something cold and wet roughly nudging my hand out of the way. Bocephus then shoved his face into the closest bag. I don't know where he suddenly came from, but he was sniffing and snotting on my groceries, and I wasn't a happy camper.

"Hey," I whisper yelled. "Get your face out of my food!" As I reached down to grab the bag, the bulldog looked up at me with the remains of a package of Twinkies hanging from his mouth. I had grabbed three of the two packs at the checkout as an impulse purchase. Drooling excessively and spitting out the plastic wrapper as he gulped down the golden treats, Bocephus licked his lips with an unnaturally sizeable forked tongue and spoke. "More," the low, raspy voice said quietly. Emboldened or annoyed by my stunned silence, he got louder and repeated, "MORE!" His lips never moved when he opened his mouth, but the sound came out, nonetheless. Steam puffed from his flaring nostrils as he spoke.

A little bulldog followed me back to my apartment, assaulted my groceries, and demanded more Twinkies in a voice that sounded like the late James Earl Jones had swallowed a handful of dirt. That was certainly unexpected. I've seen a few surprising things in my twenty-eight years of magic. A talking dog has not been among them.

I stood there for a moment to contemplate what was happening. "You just spoke to me."

"Mmmm, good," was the gruff response.

"You're a dog. A little brown dog with too many wicked pointy teeth and a forked tongue, and you spoke to me."

"MORE?" It was a question this time, almost polite in the asking as his head cocked sideways in the way only a dog can do.

The moment of revelation slapping me in the face was almost as palpable as the first time my Nana heard me swear. Granted, I was only 7, but I never said that word again until after she died. Most people would probably have run from the scene as quickly as possible, yelling about a furry demonic dog. I simply recognized the moment as one filled with signs of magic and made what could have been an exceedingly stupid decision.

I twisted the key in the lock and flung the door open, telling the snack-stealing talking canine, "Get up these stairs before someone sees you or, even worse, hears you!"

At that moment, the headlights of a passing car flicked across the two of us, and I momentarily saw the enormous dragon shadow stretched against the brick wall of the building. A shadow that only a true fire-breathing dragon who shouldn't be standing on Main Street could cast. In a flash, I surmised the animal was not only magic but also not of this ordinary twenty-first-century world. Call me stupid, but it made sense at the time. I let the little fella scoot inside and shut the door behind me.

What do you do when a giant, scaly, winged dragon in the form of a bulldog shows up at your apartment and decides he will hang out with you and eat your groceries? You roll with the punches, as they say. Magic isn't always predictable, and you don't always get a choice.

"Now what?" I thought to myself. I've got to work the breakfast shift in the morning, and suddenly, I'm in my third-floor apartment with a talking dog that seems to secretly be a dragon, if we can predict by that shadow. Magic life is brimming with unexpected moments, that's for sure. I found myself more intrigued than frightened. Magic can seep into the cracks and wrap itself around you. In a world filled with ordinary days, it's not bad to have an extraordinary one occasionally, even if that extraordinary day includes a dragon who really, really likes Twinkies.

"What's life without a few dragons?"
Ron Weasley, Harry Potter and the Goblet of
Fire

Chapter Three

An Extraordinary Tuesday

I have a job waiting tables at a restaurant down by the river. My workplace has a beautiful view in the summertime with lots of outdoor tables overlooking the rushing water on its way to the sea. The job is not without its share of mishaps that require my intervention. Yesterday, another server's tray started to tip, and I saw a bowl of hot soup nearly slide into a sweet little old lady's lap. Miss Kittles was my second-grade teacher, and I have a soft spot in my heart for her. One day, I remember her telling me, "You're different from the other kids, Wilder. You think about things differently than the other boys and girls. You'll find your place in the world someday, and it will be special." With a little magic push, I set everything level again and averted a near disaster. I know it doesn't seem like much, but I'm confident I saved her a significant degree of pain and maybe even a visit to the hospital. Small things to help people, that's my goal. I like having karma on my side.

Tuesday was perfectly ordinary on the outdoor patio. A dozen customers were enjoying their lunch in the early summer sun, and we had plenty of staff working. That's not always the case because three employees stopped showing up for work just last month. Nobody knows why, but after what I saw in the river later that afternoon, I suspect the people serving lunch became lunch for something else.

The midday sun made those little star reflections off the water as the river flowed lazily past the parking lot below the dining patio. The apartments and condos in the renovated old mill building across the river have a fantastic view. The residents never need a sound machine at night. The soothing noise of that water flowing by would help lull almost anyone to sleep like a baby. In between customers, I sometimes stand at an empty table near the railing to enjoy the view while rolling more silverware inside napkins. A restaurant can never have enough of those.

Toiling away and staring at the stars on the water below, I was surprised to see a head pop out of the water's surface. It was no ordinary head, either. The head I saw was undoubtedly the size of a horse. Not a horse's head. I mean the entire horse. It was scaly and mottled mossy green in color, like the moss that grows on trees deep in the forest. The water trickled off the massive head as it glistened and shone brightly in the afternoon sun. Whatever body the creature had was hidden below the water except for a long iridescent tail curving up above the surface and back below the ripples like one of those fake Loch Ness Monster photos. A sea dragon swimming in the Saco River wasn't what I had expected to see on a sunny Tuesday afternoon. People who are fishing on their day off, maybe. A few condo residents who are walking their dogs along the riverbank walkway, definitely. Possibly even a handful of cormorants bobbing around on the water's surface, waiting to dive for the next meal that unwittingly swam below them. Unquestionably, I did not expect to see a dragon bobbing in the river. This was especially true since another dragon was waiting in my apartment for me to get home with dinner and Twinkies. The weirdness of my life had just doubled in an instant.

Caught off guard at the sight, I dropped a large handful of silverware with a thunderous crash, the metallic din at odds with the serene background noise of the river and traffic passing over the bridge nearby. I looked out at the sea dragon swimming in the river and then at the afternoon diners. A handful of customers looked up at me in surprise, but all quickly returned to their conversations and showed no sign of seeing anything odd. It seemed I was the only one who could see a dragon the size of a city bus now swimming in a circle only a few hundred feet away. What are the odds of two kinds of dragons simultaneously appearing in the same Northeastern city? Pretty slim, I'd bet.

"Hey, Wilder," my manager shouted from behind the outdoor bar. "Are you done with that silverware? I could use some help over here."

"On my way!" I picked up the tray of freshly rolled forks, knives, and spoons and dropped it off at the serving station.

"What can I help you with?" I asked Parker. He was an Iraqi War vet who now ran the restaurant. Red's Riverbank Restaurant has been his family's place for generations. Red is Parker's grandpa, and he still comes for lunch almost every afternoon with a few of his octogenarian friends who are still alive. They have coffee and commiserate about how much the town has changed and how much better it was "back in their day."

"I need you to carry that rack of glasses inside for me if you don't mind. It's a little too heavy for this arm." Parker had lost his left arm to an IED explosion in Fallujah. That day, he also lost four guys in his unit, which haunts him almost daily. The weight of his grief and survivor guilt can sometimes be overwhelming, and there isn't enough help for vets in his situation. His pride stops him from seeking out assistance. Living with a prosthetic arm has its own set of challenges. His device limits how much weight he can pick up, so I occasionally need to step in and help. I'm glad Parker is willing to accept a helping hand now and then.

"Nice view of the river this afternoon, don't you think?" I said, testing his response.

"Same as every other day," Parker responded thoughtfully as he looked past the parking lot at the water. He raised his hand to shield his eyes as the sun sparkles on the water flashed, the midday sun reaching its highest point in the sky for the day. "We're blessed to live in such a place instead of staring at high-rise buildings all around us." The tallest buildings in our city are just four stories, and there are only a few of them.

The sea dragon was still swimming a lazy circle in the middle of the river, so Parker obviously couldn't see it. I had to make sure, though. That's why I asked. I watched it for another few minutes until the sea dragon's head slipped below the water's surface, and with a final flick of its tail, it vanished out of sight. I wondered where it went but tucked that thought away until later.

Parker looked into the distance with a slight sideways twist of his lips as if he had a thought and dismissed it just as quickly. You could always tell when he was thinking of the war because his face got a little lost momentarily. With a quiet clicking noise out of the corner of his mouth, Parker shook off whatever crossed his mind and quietly said, "Lots to get done this afternoon," as he walked away.

As I returned to my work, Red was standing in front of me, only two feet away. He was an older version of Parker, always wearing his Veteran ball cap. His head cocked sideways, and one eye trained on me more than the other. "Lost in your thoughts, or maybe something caught your eye?" he asked me. He squinted toward the river and tilted his thinly gray-bearded chin out at the water. "Out there, maybe?"

I was taken aback at his question and must have stammered out a stupid, non-specific answer because Red let out a little chuckle. "You've worked here long enough for me to know. You're one of us."

"A military vet? No, sir. I never served. Or do you mean from Saco? I was born right here in town. Mom didn't have time to get to the hospital, and I came bursting into the world at full speed right in the kitchen."

A thick cloud passed in front of the midday sun, dimming the brightness of the day and creating deep shadows on the face of the man standing too close to me. "I don't mean neither," his Maine accent getting thicker as his voice got quieter and slower. "I mean you can see it, too." Red leaned in toward my face so close I could smell the toast and cretons he had for breakfast. The French-Canadians that live around here love it, and most restaurants don't have it on the menu.

He was silent momentarily before finally whispering, "The dragon. You were watching the sea dragon."

I stopped breathing momentarily and felt like the dining patio was a tilt-a-whirl ride at the amusement park down at the beach. For the first time in my life, someone else could see something I thought was only visible to me. My parents always thought I was making up the stories of the little forest people I saw when I was running around in the woods near our house. They chalked it up to a vivid imagination and often accused me of getting carried away in my own stories. In my tween and teen years, I gave up telling them about our woodland neighbors, and they seemed relieved to no longer have the discussions. They never would have accepted my ability to move things with my mind once that power appeared in my teens.

I took a deep breath and dove in. "Yessir, I saw it," I answered reluctantly. "I'm so glad I'm not the only one." That felt good, like releasing the valve on an over-pressurized pipe. Now, it was out there.

"It's more than just you and me, boy." Red waved a hand at his grizzled old friends. The other two men sat at their table and gave me a little nod, acknowledging that we were talking about them but not so much that other patrons might pay attention. They turned their heads back toward each other and continued their conversation.

Red went on, "You're just the most recent to join our little group. It's been more than fifty years since a new one of us showed up here, and you've been right here under our wrinkled old noses."

What is he talking about? My fingers and toes began to tingle with nervous energy, and I fought off the caveman fight or flight automatic reaction to what seemed like danger.

"I don't understand what you're saying. A new what?"

Red paused for a moment to gather his thoughts. He reached out the short distance between us to put his hand on my shoulder in a friendly manner and said, "Come back tonight. We have a poker game upstairs every Tuesday night. I'll explain it all to you then."

With that bold and unexpected statement, he turned and walked back to his friends, clapping them on the back as took his seat, and their conversations resumed with a burst of laughter. How was I supposed to return to rolling silverware after a mic drop like that?

CHAPTER FOUR

MY NAME IS BOCEPHUS

My dog obviously didn't come with the name Bocephus. There was no name tag on a collar or anything like that. When I first saw that shadow flicker against the wall, I realized he was a magical creature. It's literally a magic dragon. I considered naming him Puff at first, but then I realized how ridiculous that was, almost insulting in the very cliche nature of the idea. When we got to my apartment, a Hank Williams Jr. song was playing on the radio. The singer's nickname, Bocephus, seemed like an ornery enough name for a dragon, so it stuck. I wasn't sure if his appearance as a dog instead of a dragon was one of his magical powers or some sort of concealment spell. I needed to be careful as I tried to figure it out because if I broke the concealment spell and there was suddenly a dragon in my little apartment on the third floor, that would be kind of a big issue. Bocephus is big enough, based on his shadow, that he might knock out a wall or two. Possibly the roof, too. Bo sat on the couch watching TV while I spent the remainder of the afternoon poking around on my phone, looking for any strange legends about a dragon who could disguise himself in the form of another animal. I like to do research, but the Internet is a cesspool, as you know. Researching the magical arts means navigating a minefield of garbage websites to find something even loosely based in fact. Most of the time, those urban myths have been stretched so far from the truth that it's challenging to ascertain whether or not they ever had any authenticity.

I prefer bookstores, and I'm lucky enough to live in an area with a few good ones with lots of old books. My favorite is in Portland, up on Munjoy Hill, an older part of the city. This bookstore has stacks and stacks of tall shelves filled with musty-smelling books, including an excellent section on the occult and magic. I'm not 100% certain it is an accident that this bookstore is also right across the street from the oldest cemetery in Portland. There are tombstones dating back to before the Salem witch trials. Some of the rarer books in the store date back almost that far. Until now, most of my knowledge regarding magic has come from books since I've had nobody to teach me.

CHAPTER FIVE

GRUMPY OLD MEN

The poker table was set up when I arrived on the top floor of the old brick mill building on the river, and the men sitting around it moved to stand up with surprising quickness for their age. They all crossed the room to greet me and shake my hand, each muttering a phrase that sounded like "gratissimum novissimum custodem." Something for me to google later. They introduced themselves to me one by one. Tall and lanky Jim, with a fierce handshake that would twist the knob off a locked door. The short and hairy John Patrick stepped up, a Scotsman with flaming red hair even after eight decades on this Earth. Finally, Red grasped my right hand in both of his hands and spoke the exact phrase, pulling me toward the poker table.

"Let's play some cards and talk. We'll answer all your questions, even some you don't know you have." He sat in a wooden chair with thick outwardly curving legs that looked like it had been hand-carved for Queen Anne of England in the 1600's. Seeing how my day has been going, that's not an unlikely possibility. Jim gestured toward an empty chair, and I slid it back over the time-worn wooden plank floor to take my place at the game.

There was a substantial pile of gold coins in front of each player at the ancient dark wood table, including at my seat. The coins were each as large as a silver dollar but twice as thick. Each had strange markings in a language I couldn't read, clearly not any real currency. There were at least thirty or forty of the coins on the table in front of me. I picked one up and rolled it around the palm of my hand. It was heavy, and something about it made me gasp at the touch. The coin should have felt cool, but there was a warmth to it that spread into my skin.

"This coin is magic," I said with surprise as I carefully placed it back on the table. I couldn't believe I had just said those words aloud to another person, but in my heart, I knew these men understood.

"Aye, ancient magic. Dragon magic." John Patrick said in his rolling brogue. "It's the reason the dragon is in Saco. Draco Marinus is drawn to the treasure hidden here in our little city, laddie."

I laughed a little too loudly, but the looks I got from all three of them instantly ripped the sound from my throat. "Sorry, you're serious."

"As a heart attack, boy!" Jim's voice boomed like a cannon as he slammed his massive hairy hand on the table for emphasis, jingling the pile of coins before him. "Let's get on with the story so we can play some cards."

"What is this, a magician gang or something?" I know it sounded like a smart-ass comment, but this entire display caught me off guard. I've never met another practitioner in my whole life, let alone three of them all at once.

"Protectors, Wilder Blackwood." Jim corrected swiftly. "We aren't just magicians. There's a difference between the stage tricks and chicanery of a common magician and protecting the world from destruction by the ancient forces of dragon magic. Call me mage, wizard, even spell-caster. But never magician." He spat out the final word distastefully. "We don't do tricks for customers. We are the wizards who watch over wizards. Protectors."

"Protectors, you got it," I repeated. "What is that all about? Protecting what?"

I was told more and more of the story as our poker game progressed. I was thankful to hear it in bits and pieces because it was so fantastical and unbelievable. These three men were the last of the Thesauri Custodes, the guardians of the treasure. Their cache of magically imbued gold coins was what remained of a dragon's treasure after centuries of pilfering by men who couldn't resist the temptation of wealth. There were smaller caches of a few coins here and there around the globe, and most people didn't know what they had in their possession.

"Most of it has been melted down over the years, making many men very rich. This dragon treasure is the largest, and maybe most important, that still exists. Once you melt it down, the magic is released. Gone forever." Red looked at the pile of glittering coins in front of him. "It's our job to protect it and keep it out of nefarious hands. Someday, the magic in these coins may be needed to save the world."

Red, Jim, and John Patrick were the protectors of this, the final and most significant dragon treasure. Thesauri Custodes means "treasure keepers," and they believed I was born to be the leader of the next generation of protectors. They all had similar magical abilities to mine and had spent their lives here with one goal: Be on the watch for "revertere ad draconis," the return of the dragons.

Only two dragons are left in the magical world, and that special world is usually separated from this one. If a dragon has arrived here, something has changed in the magical world and needs to be set right. The Thesauri Custodes chose this spot long ago when the city had a different name. The settlers called it Winter Harbor, and these Protectors have been here for hundreds of years. The restaurant was first a roadside tavern, and years later, it moved into the old textile mill building. They keep the upper floors as their keep, a castle of sorts for the modern day. Red's Riverside Tavern is positioned on a hill overlooking the river with the dragon treasure hidden underneath, deep in the granite bedrock of the city. This small part of the treasure that remains above ground keeps them connected to the magical world in order to stay focused on their duty.

"Draco Marinus has arrived, so we know it's been drawn here to find the treasure," Red told me. "The sea dragon must know it's close but hasn't figured it out yet."

"If the other dragon feels the same pull, all hell is going to break loose," Jim added, standing to stretch his legs with a walk across the wide-plank floor to the window overlooking the river. "They'll fight to the death over this treasure. It's the single most important thing to a dragon."

"Let me guess," I interrupted sarcastically. "We're supposed to stop not one but two dragons from finding their treasure. Even though I never knew dragons really existed?"

"You got it right, kiddo," Red responded. "Because once that other dragon arrives, it'll be almost too late to do anything. They'll fight it out until only one survives. This city will be destroyed. Hundreds, if not thousands, will die. That dragon will use the treasure's power to rule both worlds, this one and the magical one. Neither has it right now, so it's a stalemate."

I thought about my response momentarily because I knew I was about to drop a bombshell on this little gathering. These men may be wizards, but they aren't psychic. At least, I don't think they are. I looked at each of the men in turn as I chose my words carefully, "The other dragon is already here, and he's in my living room waiting to go out and pee," I said nonchalantly , shuffling the pile of coins in front of me.

Nobody laughed. They all stared at me in silence and waited for me to talk. I reevaluated my statement and gave them the abbreviated version of the arrival of Bocephus and our last few months together.

"You're telling me Terra Draconis has been here for months, and we never knew?" Red asked quietly. "That's impossible. One of us would surely have seen it. It's a wicked big dragon!"

"Well, maybe you saw me with my dog?" I offered. "My little bulldog is apparently the Earth Dragon. He definitely doesn't act like he wants to rule the world or whatever you accused him of."

John Patrick let out a chuckle. "This isn't the time to be cheeky. I'll be mighty scunnered with this bit of stooschie really quick."

"I'm not sure what that means, or even if it's English, but I'll google translate it later. I'm telling you, it is one hundred percent true." I glanced at my phone to see how late it had become. "It's time for Bocephus to take his evening walk, so you're welcome to come along and meet him. If there's a stray cat along the way, you may even see him toast a little snack."

"But it is one thing to read about dragons and another to meet them."
Ursula K. Le Guin, A Wizard of Earthsea (Earthsea Cycle, #1)

Chapter Six

MEETING THE DRAGON

I don't live too far from the restaurant, so I usually walk to work year-round when the weather is good. The three "Protectors" kept up with me without a problem, much to my surprise. I expected to walk slowly and maybe even wait for them to catch up to me, but I was utterly wrong. These guys were as healthy as a horse and not afraid of a bit of exercise.

My apartment is on the third floor, so it has a nice view of Main Street. There's a little bar below my apartment, and I often pop in after work for a beer. It's on the second floor above the sandwich shop, and it gets overlooked by many people because it's not right on the street. That's a big bonus for the people who know about it because it gets busy but never too crowded. Tonight would probably not be one of those "drop in for a beer" nights since the whole dragon thing is happening.

I was met at my apartment door by a fast-moving dog who squeezed past me and bolted down the stairs, ignoring the men behind me. "Gotta go," Bocephus grumbled as he hit the second-floor landing and quickly turned toward the ground floor.

"Did I just hear your dog say something?" Jim asked incredulously.

"We were expecting a dragon, not a wee talking dog." The Scotsman stood in the hallway, looking down the stairs in the direction Bocephus had run, listening to the scratching at the downstairs door.

John Patrick adjusted the red and green tam o'shanter on his head and let out a slow breath. "I wouldn't be more surprised if I found a family of opossums living under me kilt."

"Gotta go!" the voice thundered, as much in our heads as out loud.

"Do you know how ridiculous that statement is?" I directed at John Patrick. "Come on, we're all going for a walk." I bounded down the steps two at a time, not waiting for the Thesauri Custodes to catch up with me. I didn't want a mess downstairs to clean up later.

"You don't even want to know how bad dragon poop smells, even when it's from a dog."

Once out on the sidewalk, Bocephus acted much like a normal dog. He sniffed and peed and walked and sniffed and peed and sniffed. You get the idea. Other than us walking, there was no pedestrian traffic on the street. The shops and restaurants were all closed, and traffic amounted to a single car every few minutes. My three new old friends trailed behind, almost as if they wanted to keep a safe distance.

"It's safe to come closer," I offered. "He doesn't bite or shoot flames at strangers."

"First time for everything," Bocephus said quietly, in his deep and rumbly voice. Did my dragon just make a joke? Nobody else heard him, and I didn't want to discuss it right now.

"Four hundred years we've been watching and waiting, and Terra Draconis looks like this and pisses on lampposts?" Red finally said. "This is not how I ever expected a mighty Earth dragon to show up."

I was surprised to find myself offended by Red's comment. He insulted a dog I didn't even have a few weeks ago, and I was ready to defend Bo.

"Well," I said thoughtfully, "If he showed up flying over the city shooting flames and scaring people, that probably wouldn't be good for anyone. This way is more low-profile."

"Dogs are good," came the gravelly growling voice, out loud and in our heads. "Like tiny dragons. Loyal, protective, fierce when they need to be."

I decided it was time to tell Bocephus what I had learned. "These three men have been waiting for you, Bo. They are ..."

"Thesauri Custodes. I know."

"Oh. Right. Sorry."

I should have realized that Bo already knew; otherwise, he wouldn't have been so brazen as to speak in front of them. Until now, I have been the only person who has talked to Bocephus. My little bulldog stopped and turned toward the men, the streetlight throwing a menacing dragon shadow up the side of the Post Office where we had crossed the street from my apartment.

"Treasure," he said as he looked up at them. "Protectors here means treasure is near."

"Aye," John Patrick responded. "The treasure." He dropped down on one knee and leaned toward Bo to quietly say, "But you don't know the biggest news of all yet, do you?"

Bo gave me a sideways glance as we all stood on the sidewalk. The occasional car that drove past probably wouldn't take note of the shadow on the building, and even if they did, it would probably be perceived as street art or something similar.

I looked down at Bo. "There's a sea dragon in the river by the restaurant." There, I said it. Simple and to the point. But I didn't expect the reaction that came next.

"I know how the birds fly, how the fishes swim,
how animals run. But there is the Dragon. I cannot tell how it mounts on the winds through the
clouds and flies through heaven. Today I have
seen the Dragon."

Confucius

CHAPTER SEVEN

TAKING WING

Bocephus reared up on his two hind legs, and the dragon shadow darkened on the wall of the Post Office. The shadow also stood on its hind legs, wings slowly flapping and neck extending to the roofline. On the ground, the Frenchie grew larger, his body now the size of the blue US Postal Service mailbox next to him. Wings extended from his back, and tendrils of smoke curled from his flaring nostrils.

"Wait, wait!" I shouted. This can't happen here on the street. "What are you doing?"

"Find dragon. Destroy."

Okay, Bo already has a plan worked out. I shouldn't be surprised. He grew more monumental and dragon-like by the second. Dramatic movie music played in my head as I watched him transform from a pudgy, flat-faced dog into the fiercest creature I'd ever seen. The streetlights flickered off his red-hued scales as Bo reared toward the sky, his hind leg muscles tensing as his upper body swayed. He was enjoying this moment in his proper form, freed from the restraints of being a tiny dog.

Bo flicked his long tail, smacking into the side of the street mailbox and making it ring with a metallic ka-chang like a dull gong. It would have been louder if not for the white hairy tip of the tail, matching the long white beard on his chin. His back is ridged with a row of bony upright plates, not unlike a stegosaurus, each colored deep scarlet. His two front legs are thick and heavily muscled, matching the rest of his leathery, scaly body. The scales aren't smooth but have a rough texture, like overlapping shingles. Bo has four massive wickedly sharp claws on the end of each leg, front and rear, long and seemingly sharp enough to tear a large animal apart with a single blow.

Steam rose from his two flaring nostrils as Bocephus sniffed the air, searching for the scent of his nemesis.

"There it is," Red said with tears in his eyes. "Terra Draconis, right in front of the US Post Office in Saco, Maine."

"Speak politely to an enraged dragon," Jim said quietly, almost to himself.

"Quoting Tolkien stories, are we?" John Patrick laughed. "We've got legends about dragons in Scotland; most of them are true, and none of them are good news for us. The beithir almost had me once, but I was ready with water and a snake's head in my goat-skin bag."

I looked at him incredulously, and John Patrick saw the confusion on my face.

"Don't ye know anything, lad? Ach, we have so much to teach and so little time to get it done."

Bo's wings flapped slowly in the evening air, like a butterfly who had just hatched from the cocoon and was waiting for them to air-dry before taking flight. He craned his neck toward us, as tall as the streetlight now illuminating him in all its bright energy-conserving LED glory. He snorted a puff of smoke toward us, but not in a challenging or defiant way. "I. Am." Bocephus said in a deep, rumbling voice, louder and more bombastic than before, if that's even possible. "DRAGON."

Cue the dramatic movie music because this is too wild even to be happening.

He stretched upward on his powerful muscular back legs, digging his claws into the sidewalk for a grip as he prepared to leap for the sky. The cement crumbled to bits under Bo's feet as he dug in. His enormous leathery wings flapped slowly, stirring up enough wind to knock over the recycling bin down the street and setting off a whirlwind of litter in the middle of Main Street. Then, with a massive push and a whoosh of displaced air, he was gone, effortlessly lifting beyond the streetlights and rooftops into the starlit sky.

We have been together for just over three months, but I've never seen his true form other than as a shadow. This transformation is as new to me as to the more worldly and experienced men standing nearby. I was every bit as mesmerized and astonished at this bit of shock and awe as the Thesauri Custodes. That's a freaking dragon slowly circling the City Hall clock tower.

Nobody else seemed concerned, so I was the one to say, "People are going to freak if they see that flying overhead!"

"Dragons have a way of concealing themselves from the non-magical world," Red explained. "The only thing anybody will wonder is where that sudden gust of wind came from to make the trash cans blow over. Nobody will see him until he's a dog again. He could be visible if he wanted, but dragons are wise enough to know that's generally a bad idea."

We stood there for a long time, watching Bo fly overhead. He was unmistakably getting great pleasure from his flight, circling the clock tower and darting all over the sky above town. With his wings spread wide, the massive red dragon swooped toward the street, leveling out at the last second. He glided directly down Main Street, only twenty feet above the pavement, wings stretched wide enough to almost touch the lamp posts on either side of the street. Bo flew low enough that one flap of his wings would take out a streetlight or two, but he was cautious in his flight. With an upward twist of his neck, his body began to gain altitude over the roadway. With one mighty flap, he was a hundred feet high again, above the roof of the highest four-story building and out of sight on his hunt for the sea dragon.

CHAPTER EIGHT

PILGRIM PROTECTORS

(The following are excerpts from the journal of James Harbour, discovered in a Plymouth, Massachusetts inn that was destroyed by a fire circa 1625. It was only recently discovered during a college archeological excavation at Burial Hill in Plymouth.)

19th of December, the Year of Our Lord 1620. It was only yesterday that we arrived in the New World. We did not reach the expected land; instead, we arrived much farther north of Virginia. We are so far removed from the territory promised to us that the men aboard are discussing a new agreement of government. They have titled it The Mayflower Compact, which I believe will serve them well.

The Scotsman and I will make our way northward still, to find a hidden place to protect the treasure we have brought from England. The trip from Southhampton was not without peril. Our seven leather-wrapped chests rest securely in the ship's hold, having been transferred from the Speedwell when she was deemed unseaworthy. I fear it was the magic imbued into the contents of our chests that nearly doomed our pilgrims' expedition to the New World.

Captain Myles Standish is well aware of the contents of our chests since he helped us prepare the dragon's coins for travel. Captain Standish will remain with the colony in Plymouth while the other six Protectors secure the remainder of the treasure in two new and heretofore unknown locations. This strange new land will provide us many years of safety, keeping the treasure far from the last two dragons. Without their treasure, the combined magical forces of the seven Protectors were able to banish them to the hidden realm. We can only pray that they will never detect the treasure and find their way back to this world.

25th of January, the Year of Our Lord 1621. Winter has been more difficult and much colder than we expected. Many of our brothers and sisters have perished, saddest of all the children. They did not choose to come to this New World. The choice was made for them. There is naught that John Patrick and I can do to change the circumstances. We use our magic to provide for the colony in as many small ways as possible. Still, after the increased number of witch trials in England in the last decennium, we are very fearful of being discovered.

There are many ways to prove one is a witch. Most people do not realize that William Shakespeare's Merchant of Venice even referred to detecting a witch when he wrote, "If you prick us, do we not bleed?" because a witch will not bleed when pricked with a needle. No one would suspect a witch would revive their dying mule in a cold barn or prevent the food in their larder from spoiling with an incantation and flick of the fingers while passing on a walk. Those are the small kindnesses we can offer whilst protecting ourselves and our extraordinarily dangerous treasure.

In the Spring, we will begin our travels along the coast to the north. We will not travel as far north as the abandoned Popham

Colony, instead staying with what may become a new colony only a day's sail to the south. A physician friend from Bideford in Devonshire, England, traveled there 3 years ago and told tales of friendly natives who greeted him with great hospitality. We believe he still lives in Winter Harbor, as he calls it. Perhaps his friendly natives can assist us. We have brought John Smith's map with us; we pray for its accuracy. We owe many debts to the explorers who came to New England before us.

We hope that Red will join us in the near future. In his last word, he was traveling to the north coast of Africa to sail with the Barbary pirates. There were rumors among the corsairs of an impossibly large sea creature dragging men from the deck of the ship to their deaths in the salty Mediterranean Sea. Men have become afraid to sail through the Pillars of Hercules, fearing the monster that can rise from the waves and set their sails alight with a single breath. Red has traveled there to ensure it is only a tall tale told by frightened sailors.

CHAPTER NINE

THE PIRATE'S FOLLY

March, 1621

As Red stood on the deck of the sturdy Barbary warship, he scanned the horizon. With the help of a magic spell, his naked eye could see more than the best Galileo spyglass the Venetians could offer. "For two weeks, I have stood on this deck," he said to the sea. "I have seen nothing and hope to see nothing evermore."

Protectors take no role in the way of many things other than as observers. Barbary pirates are raiders, slavers, kidnappers, and murderers. Hundreds of thousands of people have been enslaved, and dozens of coastal towns in Spain and Italy abandoned due to their presence in the Alboran Sea.

This part of the Mediterranean should be much busier, with ships carrying goods across the sea and fishermen working to feed their families and villages. The stories of the massive creature that appears without warning and drags ships under the waves have kept many of the fearful closer to the coast of Barbaria in the south.

"We have sailed nearly 400 leagues and seen nothing but empty sea," Red whispered to the wind and waves. "I know you're out there somewhere."

Red boarded this ship in Tripoli, deep inside the Ottoman Empire. As a red-bearded foreigner, he drew attention wherever he went. The similarly red-bearded Turk named Barbarossa ruled the Ottoman Navy nearly a hundred years ago, and the admiral's memory was fresh and legendary in the people's minds. With his long and flowing beard, Red was always noticed but never bothered as he moved about the city, consistently given the unspoken respect of being a potential descendant.

"I despise the men I am sailing with, I can barely manage to choke down the horrendous food, and I haven't had a decent drink in a month besides the piss they have in barrels below.

I should have sailed with Standish instead, but I also hate the wintertide. Mare Atlanticum is a cold and forbidding ocean, unlike the warm and welcoming air and waters here north of Barbaria."

Looking at the massive cliffs huddled over the sea near Gibraltar and Tangier, straddling the passage from the old world to the immense Mare Atlanticum, Red wondered aloud, "I may be wasting my time here, but there have been too many reports of Draco Marinus for them to be the drunken nightmares of men who have been at sea too long."

"Redbeard!" Klaas shouted at him from mere feet away. "I haven't seen you all day, and it's not a very big ship."

"That's because you've been drunk and sleeping it off in the hold," Red laughed. Klaas Kompaan was one of the few men on board with whom Red had a friendship. They were alike in some ways and different in many more. Klaas was an educated man, and their discussions were always lively and often went late into the night, long after the rest of the crew had passed out. Klaas was from the Netherlands but found his calling as a privateer in Algiers.

"I cannot deny the truth, no matter how hard the hammer pounds in my head," Klaas joked. "Why are you pacing the deck all the time, my friend?"

"I'd rather keep my eyes on the sea than my lips on the bottle," Red said, looking Klaas in the eye defiantly.

Klaas was silent for a moment, then broke out in raucous laughter.

"You must have a set of cannonballs in your breeches to talk to a man with such words of challenge. That's why we are friends," clamping a meaty hand on each of Red's shoulders.

A sudden explosion of water over the gunwale broke the men apart.

Red was thrown forward toward the foremast, catching the netted shroud before his face smashed into the unforgiving timber. The ship pitched forward, its bowsprit dipping below a wave before she righted herself. Holding tightly to the shroud, Red was more prepared as the vessel tipped backward in the wave, the stern dropping so low to the water that the captain's quarters, usually high above the waves, was brought to the water line.

The men's shouting below deck quickly became a cacophony of noise on the main deck as the ship settled in the sea, righting itself again as Red held his arms out from his body at right angles. "Sit mare tranquillitas," he spoke in a low and powerful voice, feeling the magic flowing through his body as it calmed the churning waves. Red opened his eyes, looked to the sea, and saw the dragon looking back at him.

Draco Marinus rode the waves without effort, its tail flowing and flexing behind it, the massive head high above the water. Iridescent scales glimmering brightly in the sunshine, the sea dragon straightened its head up high and blew out a gigantic long flame toward the ship. Instead of incinerating the sails with one breath, the fire burned hot above the crow's nest. The Ottoman flag burst into flames instantly, but no other part of the ship was singed. The power of having a Protector on board was evident, if only to Red and nobody else.

"Hydra!" one man shouted, as another exclaimed, "Leviathan!" There have been many names for sea dragons over the centuries, and these men have heard them all. Not a single man on board is excited to see it in person, and most are busy pissing their breeches. They expect to be dragged to the bottom of the sea or eaten for lunch by the creature whose head is higher above the sea than the mizzenmast.

Ignoring the shouts of the men around him, Red walked to the rail at the edge of the main deck. "Come on, me bucko. Let's have a good look at ye."

As if responding to Red's wish, the sea dragon curved its long neck toward the deck as water trickled down the rest of the dragon's long and scaly body. As it leveled above the water directly across from Red's position, the dragon turned and looked at the man, snuffing hot smoky air from the two flaring nostrils at the end of its snout.

"The sea belongs to me," the dragon hissed in a deep and watery voice. "A single wizard against the mightiest creature in the ocean. Do you think your sword can harm me? You are as out of place here as a man flying in the sky. I could crush you with a single breath, and no one would even know this ship existed."

Men fled the ship to try and save their own lives, jumping off the opposite side and into the waters of the sea. They were too far away from shore to be able to swim to safety, so they were only delaying their moment of death. Red's hands glowed with power as he attempted to save the ship from damage. His fingers were splayed wide, encircling the ship in a protective spell and preventing the sea dragon from touching the vessel.

Draco Marinus leaned toward Red, facing him directly and stopping merely a few feet from the powerful Protector. The air between them shimmered and flickered with magical energy as they tested each other, sending out mental feelers and probing for strengths and weaknesses. It was a test of fear and fortitude as much as a test of power.

Red did not back down. Time seemed to stand still, and the remaining men on the deck were mesmerized by the scene, no longer able to flee. With a grunt and snort of smoke from flared nostrils, the dragon reared back and extended its head toward the sky, releasing an ear-splitting shriek followed by a massive long flame directly overhead. The sound rebounded off the cliffs marking the Pillars of Hercules, bouncing from one continent to another until the echo died away. Eyes locked on Red, the sea dragon slipped below the water's surface without another sound, barely making a ripple as it disappeared.

"Someone on this ship has kept a few tales to himself," Klaas said with a half-drunken laugh as he stepped from behind a longboat on the main deck where he had been hiding. "Let's grab a bottle, and you can tell me a few stories."

CHAPTER TEN

I AM AN IDIOT

Valerie makes the best sandwiches, but that's not the only reason I get lunch from the sandwich shop downstairs a few days a week. I don't want to show up every day because it'll be too obvious that I have the hots for her.

She turned as the bell on the front door tinkled, signaling the arrival of a new customer. The inside of this store probably hasn't changed much since her grandfather opened it in the 1950s.

"Wilder! It's been a few days since you were in for a sandwich. Anything exciting and new happening in your life?"

More than you can even imagine, I thought. "Nothing in particular," I said instead. "Same old, same old."

"Same old ham and cheese Italian sandwich with salt, pepper, and oil, then? Or are you going to shock me and order something different?"

I must have ordered the same sandwich a hundred times over the last few years. It wasn't that I particularly loved the sandwich or didn't like what else was on the menu. The rest of America calls it a hoagie, but here in Maine, it's called an Italian sandwich. An Italian sandwich takes her a few extra minutes to make, and those are minutes we can spend talking as she works in front of me, slicing the tomatoes, green peppers, onions, pickles, and olives.

"Why change a good thing?" I responded.

"Sometimes a good thing can be right in front of a person and they don't even seem to know it," she said as she avoided my eyes.

Was Valerie outright flirting with me? I could feel my breath quickening and the beads of sweat forming on my forehead.

I was stymied for a minute, not sure how to respond. "I uhhhh ..."

Valerie looked at me for a minute, waiting for a more intelligent response. When one didn't come, she continued.

"Those whoopie pies on the counter are fresh; they just were delivered this morning. You should have one with your lunch."

Maybe I thoroughly misunderstood what was happening here. At first, it seemed like she was flirting with me, but her following comment about the whoopie pies made it seem completely innocuous.

Valerie smiled at me again, "Let me know if you see anything else you're interested in."

There is no way my life is turning into a rom-com. I must be taking her comments out of context. Here I am, acting like a total moron while the prettiest girl in town is flirting with me. My brain began yelling at me, "Say something that isn't stupid," but no words came out of my mouth even though my lips were opening and closing like a fish out of water.

She finished wrapping my sandwich and turned to face me. "Lunch is on me today, Wilder." Valerie grinned as she tilted her head slightly and looked at me coyly, "Maybe someday you can return the favor for dinner."

There it is, no mistake this time! What has happened in my life for something so amazing to happen to me? I've thought about asking Valerie out for over a year and couldn't get up the nerve. I must have waited too long to answer because her face fell slightly.

"Maybe not," she said. "I'm sorry if I was too forward." She was crushed. Now I've really done it by not answering quickly enough, and she'll never go out with me.

"No!" I practically shouted. "No, not at all. I was surprised, that's all."

"Say it, Wilder," said the voice inside my mind. Somehow, I was finding the ability to form words, so I continued. "I'd love to take you out to dinner." I might as well go forward with honesty. "I've wanted to ask you on a date for a long time, but I didn't know if you'd be interested."

"Maybe you can tell me about that cute little dog you got," Valerie said. "I see you walking it down the street all the time. When did you get it?"

I laughed, "He just appeared at my front door a few months ago. Bo didn't have a home, so I took him in."

"Bo," she said thoughtfully. "Cute name. I bet your life has changed a bit after getting a dog."

"You have no idea," I said. "You can meet him soon."

As I turned to exit, I thought of one last question.

"Do you have any pets? A dog or maybe a cat?"

"I used to have a cat, but she disappeared a few weeks ago. It was so strange because one night, she went outside to roam around the neighborhood like always but never came back. I miss Toofie a lot."

I did not want to hear this since Bocephus also likes cats, except in a very different way.

"Umm ... what's up with the name? Toofie?"

"Yeah," she laughed. "When I got her, she was missing a front tooth. So that's what I named her. It seemed to fit."

"Well, I hope she turns up," I said with a smile, knowing that wouldn't happen. "How about if I check my work schedule for next week so we can make dinner plans?"

"I love it," Valerie responded. "I like the dragon, by the way."

I almost dropped my sandwich and fell over my own two feet at that comment.

"What?" It's impossible for her to know about Bo, right? He looks like an ordinary dog. With all that dragon magic, nobody can even see his transformations.

She gave me a puzzled look, then laughed at my reaction. "The Dragon Chinese restaurant on the corner over the bridge. They have the best General Tso's chicken. Maybe we can go there."

My heart was hammering in my chest, and my head was spinning. This conversation is too much craziness for me to handle.

"Of course!" I said, taking in a deep breath. "That sounds perfect. General Tso's chicken sounds delicious."

My life has unquestionably turned into a rom-com.

"Once a man has seen a dragon in flight, let him stay home and tend his garden in content, someone had written once, for this wide world has no greater wonder."

George R.R. Martin, A Dance with Dragons

CHAPTER ELEVEN

VOICES IN THE TREES

16 years ago

Running through the woods makes me feel unstoppable. Dodging downed trees, flicking low-hanging branches aside, and leaping over every obstacle in my path, I careen through the woods behind my house. Pushing my way through nature's obstacles without getting injured was enough of a challenge since my mom wouldn't be thrilled with me. Doing it without making a sound was even more onerous.

I silently sped through the verdant landscape, relishing every obstacle that presented itself. Other kids in the sixth grade like to run cross-country for the middle school team, but I prefer to run solo. My friends like to screw around too much, not taking the runs seriously. They quit halfway through to go to KFC for a bucket of chicken or stop at someone's house for an hour of video games before resuming their run. That's no way to get better. I want to be the fastest kid in school. I like to run so fast that I feel like I'm flying.

There are days when I feel like the leaps over rotting tree trunks crossing my path are almost effortless. I imagine I'm barely jumping as I run, but I'm still getting more air than Michael Jordan. Sometimes, it seems like I'm moving so fast my feet barely touch the ground.

A small field of fat wild blueberries is in a clearing a few hundred yards into the woods, and I was headed there to pick some. As I approached the area this afternoon, I ran my hardest, jumping and dodging underneath the canopy of trees, pushing myself through the woods at a breakneck speed I didn't even know I was capable of. It's almost as if I was being propelled by an unseen force, like a wind that I can't feel. Breaking out into the clearing, the sudden warmth of the sun on my face made me stop in my tracks, basking in the warm sunshine after the cool, damp air of the forest.

I breathed in deeply, filling my lungs with the crisp morning air and enjoying the pounding of my heart after that run. I was suddenly concerned that I was trampling some of the bushes in my favorite spot to pick blueberries, so I looked down at my feet. I wasn't stomping on any bushes or leaving any trace of my passing at all.

Somehow, my feet weren't even touching the ground. For an instant, I saw my shoes hovering above the bright green growth at the edge of the trees, a good ten inches above where they should have been planted firmly on the ground. I collapsed, feet suddenly crashing to the ground. My knees buckled under the sudden drop, and I fell to my side, momentarily confused by what I had just seen. I hadn't imagined it. I had been running without even touching the ground. No wonder I had been able to move so fast.

As I lay there on the soft grassy field, cool moss pressing into my cheek as the sun glared into my eyes over the top of the tall clover and grass surrounding me, I heard them. Multiple voices, all laughing quietly. I sat up with alarm. Silenced by my movement, there was no noise except for the wind whispering through the leaves in the treetops.

A few seconds later, the whispers began. I could hear voices, but not in a language I understand. I was only twelve, so I didn't know any foreign languages except for a few words in French, and those were mostly swears.

I stood up slowly, knocking the detritus off my shirt and legs from the grassy field. I let my eyes wander across the clearing, searching for movement. I didn't feel afraid or nervous. My breathing had slowed from my run, and I was calm as I looked out over the open area. Without a sound, a head popped up above the grass mid-field. I had the impression that the figure was standing, not crouched in the grass. If that were true, it would make the creature no taller than my dad's waist.

As it stood, I watched without reacting. Quietly, another stood up, then another. Within two minutes, seven little people stood fifty feet away from me in the clearing. I wondered whether they were tiny men or spirits of the forest. Merely seconds later, I got my answer. One of the small forest people stepped towards me through the blueberry bushes. The man was shorter than me, perhaps three or four feet tall. He had brown skin and black hair with a long white beard. Dressed in animal skins that covered his midsection, the rest of his body was bare. He spoke in a language I did not understand with my ears but was as easily understandable in my head as my own mother's voice.

"We are the Mikumwess, and this is our forest. You are welcome here," he gestured with his hands to the trees surrounding us.

"I have run through these woods so many times, why haven't I ever seen you before?"

"You were not ready, but now you have grown. You are special, and different from the others in your tribe. We do not wish to be seen by them."

"I'm not special, I'm just a kid who lives over there," I pointed toward my house.

I didn't know what to think. I have been running and playing in these woods for years. I'd never seen another person, let alone a tiny forest creature. I suppose it could be my over-active imagination. That's definitely what my dad and mom would say. This was real, though. I knew it. In the middle of the woods, not far from my house and my grandparents' house, were the seven little people that look a bit like Native Americans. Maybe they are related somehow.

"You are not the same as the rest. We call you Runs-On-Air when we see you pass through our land."

"Oh, that! I didn't even realize until today," I replied sheepishly. "I don't even know how that happened."

A few of the Mikumwess laughed at my comment, making me slightly embarrassed.

Shushed by the first speaker, who seemed to be a leader of this group, they quieted right away.

"We are always here if you need us. We can help you when others do not understand your differences. Always remember us, we are the spirits of the forest."

They all turned in unison and ran across the clearing. Seven tiny figures vanished quickly into the cover of the brush and woods, moving without making a sound.

Chapter Twelve

FIRST FLIGHT

Flying on a dragon's back has never been on my to-do list. There are many things I have always wanted to do in my short life: learn to play guitar, go scuba diving, and compete on a reality TV show like Survivor, which I always used to watch with my parents. I'd be the most popular contestant because I could scuba dive to catch fish, cook them over a fire I started with a flick of my fingers when nobody was looking, and then entertain everyone at night with a few campfire ukelele songs.

I'm much too shy to do anything like that, but I've thought about it plenty of times.

Bo likes to explore the area during the day as a dragon instead of at night as a dog. A dragon cannot be seen unless it wishes to be seen. Through magic no others understand, a dragon has the ability to remain invisible to the naked eye of anyone except another practitioner of magic. Even a dragon cannot hide the physical effects of it presence, though. It's easy enough to explain away garbage cans knocked over by a sudden gust of wind or cats and dogs that go missing in the middle of the night. More problematic still are the random fires and puffs of smoke that seem to appear out of thin air. The sudden noise and powerful slam of a heavy object hitting the ground, even when there is nothing anywhere in sight, is unexplainable. Nobody ever says, "Hey, was that a dragon landing?" A dragon flying past still produces wind, and even the softest landing by a Terra Draconis can be felt blocks away when the ground shakes from its weight.

We were on one of our regular walks on a beautiful sunny Maine afternoon when Bo stopped dead in his tracks. "Morphing time," he chuffed. I need to turn off the TV when I leave the apartment. A dragon being influenced by Power Rangers can't be a good thing.

"Now? Here?" I asked incredulously.

"No houses, no people," he responded. We were on a curve in the road, out of sight from any of the nearby homes. We had passed houses with kids playing in the front yard, people mowing the grass, nanas pulling weeds from their flowerbeds, and retired old men sitting on the front porch watching the world pass by. This section rounded a bend crossed by railroad tracks, away from any eyes that might witness something they thought was impossible.

"But where are you ..." I was too late for questions. Within seconds, I stood next to an enormous red dragon, wings shaking themselves loose and flapping slowly over my head.

"Get on. Let's go," Bo growled at me. His long neck craned toward the road, his face almost level with mine as his glittering gold-flecked eyes stared at me.

"Get on? Do you mean your back? Like I'm riding a horse?" My heart started to pound faster.

"Too many questions," came the huffy response. "Do it. I triple-dog dare you."

There's another example of TV rotting the brain of an 800-year-old dragon.

Bocephus extended his front leg and lowered his shoulder down toward the pavement. I stepped up and reached over my head for one of his neck spikes. Using it as a handle, I pulled myself up and threw my right leg over the other side. Surprisingly, there was a perfect spot between the armored plates to sit, and I could settle in somewhat comfortably and hold two spikes to maintain my balance.

"I'm as ready as I'll ever be. Let's go before I chicken out," I spat out with zero confidence. I tried my best to stop the slight tremble that had developed in my legs. I didn't want my dog to make fun of me.

Bo squatted slightly on his haunches, back legs preparing to spring upwards. We launched into the air a moment later, already higher than a telephone pole with one leap. A few flaps of his wings later and we were over the houses, every resident inside unaware of what was happening overhead.

As we soared higher and higher, the view below transformed into a vibrant quilt of colors, a patchwork of shingled rooftops, green gardens, and winding streets, all glowing under the golden embrace of early summer sunshine. Down below, I could see people working in their yards, mowing the lawn, or walking their dogs. Thanks to the dragon's magic, none of them could see the enormous dragon cutting through the sky, scales shimmering in shades of red unlike any other creature in the sky. They certainly didn't witness the rider, knuckles clenching what passed for handles on a dragon's back, turning as white as the clouds.

I could feel my heart racing in my chest and the blood pulsing in my ears as we climbed higher and higher. No matter how tightly I held on to Bo, I couldn't be sure if the shaking in my hands came from the wind and cold or from the terror I felt perched atop an impossible beast capable of incinerating any of the homes below in a split second of fiery breath. The cool air chilled my skin as it sliced through my hoodie. The air whipped against my face, causing tears to stream down my cheeks. At least, that's what I told myself was the cause. In truth, it was probably the intense rush of exhilaration, the wild thrill of the dragon's mammoth mighty wings beating against the sky, and the freedom of flying without a care in the world. The thrill I felt at that moment was unlike any other feeling I've ever had, and I let the emotion take over. Every tiny shred of fear that surfaced was overwhelmed by the sheer joy of the experience.

The clouds above my head seemed close enough to touch as they gleamed in the sunlight, every molecule of water vapor shining against the blue backdrop. With each mighty flap of Bo's wings, we raced across the sky, diving and soaring with abandon. I could see the Saco River snaking its way to the ocean, shimmering like a wide ribbon of silver in the sunlight as it cut through the landscape. Bo was enjoying this flight as much as I was. At that moment, I could feel the emotional connection that had formed between us, a bond unlike anything else in the world—dragon and rider, spell-caster and familiar.

CHAPTER THIRTEEN

HIDING THE TREASURE

(Winter Harbor, Maine June 1621)

When John Patrick and James, as he was known then, arrived in Winter Harbor, they were happy to be well-received by the settlers and the local natives. The natives had helped the settlers adapt to their new surroundings and even went so far as to assist them in planting crops, hunting and fishing, and building shelters. The two men had brought the chests of treasure to hide away, and their first duty as Protectors was to find a location that would keep the treasure safe for years to come .

"James, the location we seek must be impenetrable and hidden so well that no temptation will be sufficient to make us want to exhume the chests from their hiding spot easily."

"The Sokoki Indians know the river better than we can ever hope," James replied to John Patrick. "We will use their knowledge for our benefit. First, we must cast the spells to gain their trust and assistance and allow them to forget forever what they assisted us with."

The rocky river bank in was riddled with small caves, most too small to be of any use to the men, and some only pockets in the rock that didn't provide any shelter or cover. They would need a larger space to hide their four chests of dragon treasure, but not a space large enough to provide easy access. Days were spent searching up and down the banks of the river, in and out of coves and inlets on its banks. Finally, one area on Indian Island stood out better than the rest, an accidental discovery that surprised even the natives. It was a tiny cavern twenty feet above the river on a steep granite face, difficult to access and nearly hidden from view by the surrounding rocky outcropping.

Once inside the small cavern, however, a divining spell cast by John Patrick found an enormous cave just beyond a thin wall of granite.

James knew how to proceed best. "We can carefully use our magic to break through this stone, thus exposing the greater cave beyond. When we have finished moving the chest into the cave, we will rebuild and reseal the wall. Even if this small cavern is discovered high above the water, no one will ever detect the cave's existence beyond this space."

A concentrated spell from both men simultaneously was necessary to chip through the granite wall between the smaller and larger caves. Not unlike picking away at the stone with a prospector's ax, their spell broke through bit by bit, leaving a pile of stone chips on the cave floor as they made their way into the destination cave. It only took a few hours, whereas Indians working with pick-axes would have taken days to break through.

Under cover of night, the natives helped bring chests to the river below the small cave entrance. Using ropes, they assisted the men in hoisting the heavy chests into the small cave above and then through the entrance James and John Patrick had created.

The Protectors felt some guilt using the other men in this manner, but it was the only way they could move the chests into a concealed place without future fear of the treasure ever being discovered or removed. Convincing good men to do their bidding and forcing them to forget did not seem like a Godly decision, but they could see no other way.

A re-weaving spell was all it took to rebuild the section of stone that had been chipped away. Easier to restore than to destroy, the bits and pieces of stone flew into place, the new rock every bit as strong as it had begun.

Once the four chests were tucked away, the Protectors set about to create new lives in this settlement. They built a tavern and roadhouse overlooking the island in the middle of the river, providing them with a vantage point unlike any other to keep watch over the treasure for many years to come. The island, known to the colonists as Indian Island, was the primary settlement for the Sokoki tribe. Another Abenaki tribe had a large village nearby in Winter Harbor, only a few miles away.

The settlers were excited to have this tavern in their growing new town. Until the tavern was open, there hadn't been a place for the townspeople to gather and discuss the important topics of their new lives here. The settlement was still small but growing a bit every month. With each bit of new growth, new problems were arising. Many felt it was essential to continue with a plan and structure for the village instead of allowing random development. This became apparent when a small group of men began to raise timbers on their new pig barn next to the church. It was a simple matter that no other townspeople wanted to be next to that during their worship. Even the other farmers were in agreement.

John Patrick, always looking for a new laugh, came up with the idea to name the new establishment.

"Let's name it after Red, and he'll get a laugh out of that when he joins us from his adventure with the Barbary pirates hunting for sea monsters!"

Red's Riverside Tavern quickly became the gathering spot for the village and a vital lookout for the Protectors to oversee the location of the dragon treasure, now buried deep below them in a hidden cave.

One early fall afternoon, the tavern door opened to a familiar face standing in the doorway, and a boisterous voice echoed across the room.

"I see I'm too late to assist you gentlemen with your tasks. My apologies! Rest assured, now that I have arrived, your worrying days are over."

"George, you old scoundrel! The only worry we have now is you drinking all of the beer! We expected you months ago," James said as their friend walked through the front door. "Let me pour you a whistle-belly, and we'll tell each other of these last few months."

Moving toward one of the long, rough-hewn wooden tables that filled the center of the room, John Patrick sat on a bench on one side, leaving the other side of the table to their old friend. James poured a molasses and sour beer for each and joined them, raising a toast to reunited friends.

"That's an offer a man can't say no to," George said with a laugh. "My throat was as dry as an old fish while traveling here! Someday, you'll learn how to brew a proper beer!"

"Our barley crops should do well next year," John Patrick asserted. "In the meantime, the locals have taught us how to make beer with their maize. It will be ready for drinking next week. They tell us the water is pure, but most of the settlers in the village dinnae want to take the chance. Yer lookin' a bit peely wally, drink up!"

The first beer disappeared quickly, and the conversation between the men flowed as easily by the third. The old friends hadn't seen each other in months and had much to catch up on.

George began to fill them in, "I most recently came from Plymouth Colony. Much has changed since you left in the spring. I assisted the good people in making friends with the local Indians. They call themselves the Wampanoag Nation. Their chief, Massasoit, is a sagacious man. I believe they are planning a celebration of their peace in the coming months. Only two score and ten persons survived the winter, and they are eager to learn from the friendly tribe."

Setting his empty tankard on the table with a thud, John Patrick laughed. "Ha ha, it's good the local Indians are also friendly to us here. Otherwise, we'd have had no help at all securing our chests in a proper spot since you took so damn long to get here."

"I hate to be the bearer of bad news, but I have something to tell you gentlemen."

Recognizing a serious turn in the conversation, James and John Patrick placed their hands on the table, palms down. All eyes were now on George the Protector.

'I have spent many years in service to our cause, but now is the time for me to step away. I have fought dragons, built villages, assisted kings and noblemen, and worked alongside the best men God ever created. I have used my special abilities to improve the world for hundreds of years, so help me God."

He paused to wait for a reaction. When John Patrick nodded understandingly, George continued.

"Now I yearn for a quiet cabin and a field to plow, to watch my children grow and to look forward to life, not over my shoulder. I will not be far away. I promise you men I will always be close enough to help you if the time ever arises."

George pushed back from the table and stood ramrod-straight, looking down at his friends.

"Until I take my dying breath, I will serve the Protectors. There shall never be another dragon to threaten this realm, and the Earth will be a place of peace and harmony. God be with you both," and he walked out the door into the early summer sunshine.

"We should not be just a fan of dragons; we should always be the dragon himself. Then we will not be afraid of any dragon."

Shunryu Suzuki

CHAPTER FOURTEEN

THE CHOICE IS MADE

The last light of the day beamed through the window on the west side of the room, sharing the warm glow of sunset with the bare wooden walls. The light slanted low, filling the room with the light of the golden hour. Beyond the window, the Saco River wound through town on its way to the ocean, reflecting the colors of the sunset as it concealed whatever swam beneath the surface. The room was quiet enough that you could hear the faint hum of traffic on the street below. Dust motes danced in the fading light, sparkling in the air like glitter in a movie magic spell. Each shimmering and floating like tiny, weightless stars in the fading sunlight. One could easily imagine the air in the room itself was imbued with morsels of magic as the air took on a life of its own.

The three elder Protectors gathered at the heavy oak table, which had traveled across an ocean and borne witness to centuries of decisions, debates, beers and card games. They sat together now, edgy and agitated as they considered the future of their positions and the new Protector that had joined their group, turning their trio into a quartet. The arrival of the dragons had turned their future into one that was less certain than it had been for hundreds of years.

"Why didn't anyone bring food for this meeting?" Jim said. "I'm starving!" He was always hungry. Considering how lanky he is, Jim must have the metabolism of a teenager to burn off the calories.

"You'll be fine for an hour, Jimmy-boy. Then we'll go downstairs and eat," Red replied. "Stop being an 800-year-old baby."

John Patrick continued gruffly, "This is a pivotal moment for the Protectors. It's been nae a lang time since we welcomed a new member. Are we sure he's got what it takes to make sure the treasure is secure, or are our heads full of mince?"

"I have no doubt," Red responded thoughtfully. Standing up from the table, he walked across the wooden plank floor to the window. "I've known this boy for years. Customers and coworkers at the restaurant are clueless about his casual magic, and I've witnessed some trickery that would be difficult for a less-talented mage. Sometimes, he tosses out spells without even a hitch in his step, as if he was swatting away a fly in the air."

"The only way we're going to defeat that big green beastie is with some trickery of our own." John Patrick added. "D'ya think we can get the wee dog to help us? There's an old Scottish saying: Guid gear comes in sma' bulk."

"Good things come in small packages, yes. I have a few ideas about that," Red began, turning from the window to face his comrades. "We need to get the sea dragon to return to the other side and away from this realm. There's too much danger for this world if we don't succeed. Those two dragons are ready to claim their territory, and many lives will be lost in the process."

Red returned to the table and sat down, rejoining his friends. Placing his elbows on the worn wooden surface, he folded his hands and looked at John Patrick and Jim.

"Tell me what you think about this idea I am about to share with you."

# CHAPTER FIFTEEN

THE TRUSTED KNIGHTS

The next evening, the Protectors all gathered together to explain the plan to Wilder. Gathered around their ancient table on the top floor of their modern-day keep overlooking the river, the men began the story at the very beginning.

"The first Thesauri Custodes came together in the Middle Ages when dragons were more common and feared by kings and commoners both," Jim explained to Wilder. "When they first began to defeat the dragons and collect the magical treasure, there was a need for a more official organization in order to work together better. That's how the Thesauri Custodes was born, the treasure keepers."

Red and John Patrick sat nearby, listening to Wilder's questions and often interjecting when they thought Jim omitted some vital detail.

"We aren't the first, and you won't be the last!" Red told Wilder. "We are simply the latest in a long line of treasure keepers, all alive longer than any other humans to keep the treasure safe."

"Quit yer haverin',' Now it was John Patrick's turn. "It's part of the treasure's magic. It extends a protector's life span. We aren't immortal and certainly not invulnerable. But any dunderheid knows we live a lot longer than most!"

Jim continued his story for Wilder. Most dragons had been defeated by 1600, and their treasures all collected together and hidden away in various parts of the world, never keeping too much of it together in one place to attract attention from "beyond the veil" where the Thesauri Custodes had banished the remaining dragons.

"I have a big question that's been bothering me," I said. "You have all been alive for hundreds of years."

"I'm almost 500 years old," Red replied as he jumped up. "But I don't feel a day over 70!" They all laughed as he held his back and pretended to limp around the room.

"What's your question, son?" Jim asked.

There was something Wilder had been considering for a few weeks now. It seems apparent that the aging process was slow for the Protectors, but where did the money come from to support their everyday lives?

After he posed the question, Jim answered with another story.

"Many years ago, back at the beginning before the years were accounted for, King Arthur called the founders of our Thesauri Custodes into action. There was a dragon menacing the commoners near Cardinganshire in the Welsh countryside. The king sent a message to one of his Knights of the Round Table, Sir Piedge Exrog. He was a trusted knight of the king who lived in his family's castle at Cardmore at Cardinganshire. Whitney Castle stood on the banks of the River Wye, on a spit of gravel at the river's bend."

"Wait a second," I interrupted. "King Arthur was real?"

"Ya can do magic with barely any extra thought and have a dragon living in yer apartment, but ya question me about King

Arthur? Are ya daft, lad?" John Patrick laughed boisterously, taking a swig from his glass.

"Fair point," I said. "Please go on."

As Jim continued to share his story, the room fell respectfully silent.

"Fairy tales are more than true: not because they tell us that dragons exist, but because they tell us that dragons can be beaten."

Neil Gaiman, Coraline

In the Beginning

"Sir Peidge Exrog was a Knight of King Arthur's fabled Round Table and one of the greatest warriors in the court. More than that, he was one of the earliest Protectors and the founder of our secret order that has lasted for centuries. In the beginning, Sir Exrog was called by the king to vanquish a dragon that had been terrorizing his subjects in the hills. Assembling a handful of gallant knights and brave noblemen, they sought out the ancient dragon that had emerged from a cavern deep in the mountains.

The frightful dragon was unlike any that had been seen before, with scales the color of blackened iron and eyes that burned like torches in the night. The dragon had been unstoppable, burning villages and killing all those who attempted to thwart the beast's attacks.

Desperate villagers in the foothills fled their homes and fields, packing their families and meager belongings into donkey carts and abandoning everything they had worked for. Many men died as the peasants rallied together to battle the dragon to no avail. Women were left without husbands, children became fatherless, and the dragon's fiery exhalations reduced the fields to smoldering ashes.

Nothing seemed to curtail the great beast's power and rage until Sir Piedge Exrog and his companions rode into the village. They knew their biggest strength would be working together, combining their powers into a force more significant than the sum of its parts. When unified, they would be unstoppable. Each of the knights in their party had different magical abilities. Some were masters of ancient incantations that had been long forgotten. Others were able to harness the elemental forces of the Earth itself. Sir Exrog was one of the strongest wizards of all, able to call upon the powers of the ancients. He drew from those giants that had walked the land and the millennia of wizards and magical beings that had once populated the planet. None besides Merlin himself could control the mystical energies like Sir Exrog, but after this battle, he chose to minimize his place in history to lead our group.

Under the guidance of Merlin, they had crafted a marvelous plan to defeat the beast once and for all with a carefully crafted spell that would weaken the Black Dragon's invulnerability and allow the powerful small army of knights and noblemen to vanquish their enemy.

When confronted, the battle was fierce. The ground trembled and split under the dragon's attack as it scorched the battleground and burned many men in their tracks. The knights held firm, combining their powers in a way that had never been done before. Together, they were able to use their magic to form an unseen shield around them, barely feeling the heat of the dragon's torrents of flames.

Gathered in the field, they circled with swords and shields held high. As the magic intensified, the Black Dragon became weaker. The beast attempted to increase the ferocity of the attack but to no avail. Powerful blasts of flame hot enough to melt iron shot toward the well-protected group, and the dragon pounded the ground in anger. Its eyes glowed with the heat of twin suns, burning with ferocious hatred for the men it faced. The Black Dragon's tail swept left and right with ferocity, the tip ending in a cluster of thick spikes strong enough to pierce armor. Unrestrained and brutal in its attack, the beast's claws continued tearing at the earth as it strained to overpower the mighty force it now faced.

The magical protective shield surrounding them glowed brightly with power. Years later, tales were repeated and songs were written that told of the ghostly figures of ancient beings within the force field, their crystalline translucent images joining the magicians in a combined show of power the planet hadn't seen since the time of the giants.

As their chant reached a crescendo, the knights all threw their swords toward the center of the circle, where the powerful spell pulled them together into a massive magical spear thirty feet long and a man's height in diameter. The new weapon rocketed skyward, curving as it did into a trajectory toward the great beast. With a blinding flash and explosion of primordial energy drawn from the ley lines that ran beneath the men's feet, the spear pierced the Black Dragon's armored plates and thrust directly into the heart of the beast.

The fearsome creature collapsed to the ground with one last desperate thunderous roar. As the echo of that final deafening howl echoed off the mountains, the monster became still, its life force draining into the earth below. Sir Exrog, a man of great foresight, retrieved his sword and chopped three scales from the neck of the dragon. Whatever happened to those scales has faded into the mists of the past, but they are rumored to contain a portion of the great dragon's power.

Upon their return to Camelot, the king rewarded Sir Piedge Exrog and the other knights with a royal guerdon. That gift was more than just a reward. It was a symbol of their future as Protectors."

"That's a big bag of gold coins!" Red answered before Wilder could ask. "For courage and service to the crown, they used to say. The king gave the guerdon to the Lord of Whitney, Sir Peidge Exrog. The Protectors used this money for hundreds of years to sustain their way of life, and the value has grown over the centuries. That's why we ..." Red trailed off, looking around the tower room at his Protector brothers.

"Why you don't have jobs?" I finished.

"Haha, that's the short version of it!" Red laughed. "We aren't living off Social Security while protecting the land from dragons. We aren't as rich as kings, but we want for nothing.

The jobs we've held over the years are just cover for our real responsibilities."

"The skies of this world were always meant to have dragons. When they are not here, humans miss them. Some never think of them, of course. But some children, from the time they are small, they look up at the blue summer sky and watch for something that never comes. Because they know. Something that was supposed to be there faded and vanished."

Robin Hobb, Golden Fool

Chapter Seventeen

SORRY ABOUT YOUR CAR

On my days off, we like to wander the city. We started doing it even before Draco Marinus showed up, so it's killing two birds with one stone to spend the afternoon searching for any sign of him as we aimlessly roam the town's streets.

"Sometimes you look for adventure, and sometimes adventure finds you," I told Bo.

Truth be told, we could probably use a little bit less adventure and replace it with a bit of hum-drum. People go about their everyday lives, blessedly unaware of a dragon in their midst. Not only one dragon, but two. Moms and dads driving their kid to the dentist or baseball practice pass by us on the street corner as we wait for the walk light to change, and they haven't the slightest clue that the dog next to me is a real-life freaking dragon. The UPS guy stops at the crosswalk and honks, waving us across the street.

"Hey, I'm crossing as fast as I can. My dog is really dragon his feet!"

The driver couldn't hear me. I only made the joke for Bo's sake. Being a dragon, he has no sense of humor. That doesn't stop me from making lame jokes.

"Why did the dragon cross the road? Bo asks me. "To eat the cat on the other side."

I couldn't help but laugh at his weak attempt at humor. Maybe I'm wrong and he does understand humor. Nobody would expect a dragon to have jokes, though.

I heard my name called out from down the street. Looking past the post office and toward the House of Pizza, I saw Valerie on the opposite side of the street. She was waving energetically to get my attention. The way she looked as she walked toward us was enough to get my attention, I assure you. Valerie was wearing a blue dress, short enough to look sexy but still conservative enough to be a tease. It was a bit low-cut, just enough to make me want to stare. I didn't want her to think I was leering at her, so I had to be careful. This isn't something I want to mess up.

"Hold up, I'm coming over!"

She began crossing the street at the closest crosswalk but failed to look for oncoming traffic. From my vantage point, I could see the green Dodge Durango coming around the corner a little too quickly. They barely slowed at their stop sign and whipped around the corner onto Main Street. Valerie was looking at us and didn't even notice the vehicle bearing down on her.

Whispering a quick spell, I threw my left hand in the air and watched a heavy iron utility hole cover lift up in front of the Durango, only two feet above the ground. With a metallic crunch, the heavy metal disc sliced through the vehicle's front grill and into the radiator, penetrating far enough that the engine seized up, bringing the SUV to a halt.

Still focused on me and Bo, Valerie waved her hand in response, thinking I had just been waving to her. As she stepped onto the curb, she turned and saw the Dodge stopped in the middle of the street, a utility hole cover sticking out of the grille like a giant metal frisbee had been thrown into the front end.

"Would you look at that," she said to me, shaking her head as she walked up. "I wonder how that happened?"

"Must have been a sewer gas explosion that tossed the cover up into the air," I suggested. "Bad timing for that poor driver."

The driver and passenger of the Durango were out of the vehicle, standing at the front and waving their arms in confusion. Their insurance company will give them a hassle over this one, that's for sure. I didn't feel badly, though. Their misfortune saved Valerie's life. Pay attention to the stop sign next time.

Valerie touched me on the shoulder and said, "I'm on my way to the shop. Stop in for a sandwich or something, why don't you?" Patting Bo on the head, she walked off down the street.

"Are you just going to watch her walk, or are we going to keep going?" Bo could be so crass sometimes.

"Brave men didn't kill dragons. The brave men rode them."

Viserys Targaryen, Game of Thrones

CHAPTER EIGHTEEN

RIVER CHASE

Flying above the city on a dragon's back is as terrifying as you may expect. There are no seat belts on Terra Draconis. Whenever I let out a shout, Bo snorted a puff of smoke and laughed. He always enjoyed these moments. First swooping low over rooftops, then with a burst of speed jetting high into the air above the neighborhoods. People in their yards may have noticed a random momentary breeze on an otherwise windless day or wondered where the random voice shouting "slow down" was coming from. I hope no kids heard me. Sometimes, things got a little more colorful than that.

I suddenly thought of my 5th grade teacher, Mrs. Mitchell. She told my parents, "That boy always has his head in the clouds. He needs to keep his feet on the ground and stop day-dreaming all the time." Here I am now, with my head literally in the clouds. I'm flying on the back of a dragon, like people do in the movies.

Bo banked left toward the ocean. We followed the river past the marina and jetty and into the bay. Fishing boats dotted the surface of the water below, some lobstering, others looking for mackerel. The bigger catches are further out to sea. This area is plentiful in tuna, bluefish, cod, and haddock. The water is clear, with the color variances marking changes in depth. The darker it looks, the deeper it gets. The shades of blue and green below us were even more beautiful from above than they were from the ground.

"There, to your right," I shouted to Bo. We banked in that direction, getting a clearer view of the water below.

The shadow under the surface was unmistakable. I saw the long snake-like body, shaped like the letter S, under the surface and barely hidden in the small waves. "Draco Marinus," I whispered to myself.

"Going down!" Bocephus warned me, swooping toward the water in a steep nosedive.

I held on tightly as we plummeted toward the sea. Bocephus was rocketing toward the shadowy serpentine silhouette that was now below a blue and white lobster boat, twisting and writhing below the surface. Suddenly aware of our approach, the sea dragon coiled itself into a circle and thrust its head above the surface, nearly capsizing the boat. Judging by the shouting from the crew, there was no dragon cloaking magic in use, and they could clearly see Draco Marinus's head above the water, which was less than 50 feet off their bow.

Smoke bellowed from the engine compartment as the panicked captain tried to channel all of the boat's power into moving away from the unmistakable danger of the impossible creature he could see in the water. Bo swept low across the water's surface, his taloned feet dragging in the waves as we sped toward the oncoming battle. The sea dragon's body undulated under the surface as its tail came above the water and smashed down on the lobster boat, splintering the bow with a massive crash, sending the crew over the side and turtling the boat. I had to trust the lobstermen were able to get to safety, because I didn't want to spare a moment to check. There were already three nearby boats bearing down on their location.

With green scales shimmering in the afternoon sun, the sea dragon swam dolphin-like upriver. It almost seemed to be teasing Bo into a chase, which worried me as it may possibly be a trap of some kind. In and out of the water, visible for a moment above the surface and then lost below the waves for another.

Our flight was also up and down, dipping toward the surface of the water whenever Bo tried to predict the sea dragon would rise again. He repeatedly blasted the surface with flames, anticipating a glimmering green head popping up at just that moment, but he never hit the target. Steam filled the air before us as we rose high into the sky above the harbor again, searching the water below for our next sighting.

This contention between the dragons has existed for hundreds of years, according to the Protectors. As dragons were defeated one by one, it only served to fuel the hatred between those that remained. Their quest for power and possession over each other's treasure became their ultimate life goal. Finally, there were only these two dragons, and they were ready to battle here.

Draco Marinus lifted his head high above the water, most of his body visible and his tail wavering back and forth. The message was clear, "Come and get me." Bo couldn't resist the tease and dove headfirst at full speed, ready to blast and claw his enemy, defeating him once and for all.

Just as Bo released a powerful stream of burning dragon flame, the sea dragon disappeared below the waves. I was confident we'd hit the water and prepared myself to be underwater, but Bo was able to pull up in time. I released the big breath I had held for dear life as we leveled above the river, not knowing where Draco Marinus had gone. We were mid-river, with 500 feet of water on either side of us to the shoreline. Homes dotted the river's edge, and people enjoyed the summer afternoon in their yards. I could see a group of teenagers making noisy dives from a rope swing tied to a large oak branch that overhung the water. I had to remind myself that they couldn't see Bo and me, and Draco Marinus also seemed invisible to them now.

The sun shone directly above us, providing a clear view of the water and below. We were so low to the surface that Bo's claws occasionally dragged in the waves as we continued the search. As we continued upriver, I leaned over the left side of my powerful red friend for a clearer view and realized our tragic mistake.

"Pull up, pull up fast!" I yelled urgently. "Get away from the river!"

Bo was no fool and listened to his rider right away. Just as we began to rise from the surface, the sea dragon burst from directly below and attacked. The shadow below us hadn't been our own. The other dragon mirrored our flight from mere feet below the surface, mimicking a shadow and preparing to attack.

The long neck and body exploded above the river, mouth open wide with long, sharp teeth bared. The sea dragon's mouth snapped closed, missing Bo's feet and talons by mere inches as we rose into the sky. I held on as tightly as I could, braced against the armored plate behind me. With mighty wings displacing massive amounts of humid summer air and propelling us high above the river, we quickly gained altitude before Bo twisted in mid-air and dove back toward the river and his nemesis. Flames shot from his mouth as he attempted to wound the sea dragon while it was above the waterline. Draco Marinus let out a pained scream that would have given nearby residents nightmares for months if they knew the truth of this battle.

"I'm going to try something I've never done before," I warned Bo.

Daring to release my grip, I raised both hands into the air, fingers splayed wide, imagining gathering sunlight in my mind. I continued the thought, reeling in the sun's rays and storing them away somewhere inside myself. I was literally making it up as I went along. Interlocking and crisscrossing my hands between the thumbs and forefingers, I aimed my palms at the sea dragon as it passed to our right. It was bold and confident enough to still have most of its long body visible on the river's surface. This was the moment. Willing the stored energy out of my body and toward Draco Marinus, a beam of concentrated light more powerful than a laser blasted into its neck. The blinding display lasted only seconds, but it was enough to bring a terrifying roar from our attacker.

I wasn't sure if we were all visible or not, but I hoped the dragon's magic hid us from view. The last thing we needed was a bunch of tin-foil hat theorists posting on social media about a dragon battle on the Saco River in Maine. Nobody would believe it, and any photos would be accused of being generated by artificial intelligence. Government interference was danger-ous, and any interaction from that direction couldn't have a positive outcome.

As the sea dragon disappeared below the water, Bo blasted the water with flames, causing a cloud of steam to rise that almost looked like a fog bank moving in. Indeed, that would create some chatter among the shoreline residents and people in the nearby marina. A small crowd was already gathering on the docks, some with binoculars and more than a handful with cell phones pointing in this direction.

"Bo, we need to get out of here," I said. "There's more danger than just the other dragon."

The response wasn't what I expected.

"I like TV, but I don't want to be on TV," he said.

"Or a viral video!" I laughed. Most people wouldn't believe it if they saw it, and the ones who believe such a video is real don't have the credibility for anyone to take it seriously.

After our mile-long chase upriver, we almost returned to the restaurant and the city.

"Good choice," I laughed. "But where did he go? I can't see anything."

"Hiding. Waiting. He's a trickster." he responded as he slowly flapped his leathery wings and banked to the right.

"Bo," I said quietly. "What did I just do? I've never done anything like that before."

As they flew, Bo turned his head to face Wilder. The dragon's golden eyes gleamed mischievously in the bright afternoon sun, and as they began to bank to the left, he replied, "You are more powerful than you know."

We circled where we had last seen the dragon, but the water flowed from the city toward the sea as if today was a typical day on the Saco River. As the steam from Bo's fiery blasts dissipated, so did the crowd. Later that day, they would tell their friends and post on social media about the strange cloud of steam that probably came from the sewer treatment plant upriver and how it could be dangerous to the fishing industry if it weren't fixed soon. The idea would come from a particular server at a popular riverfront restaurant who tells a story so convincingly you couldn't help but believe it. A little belief magic thrown in with the story wouldn't hurt, either.

CHAPTER NINETEEN

A NEW SIGHT

Today is a typical afternoon at Red's Riverside Tavern. The sun is shining, and there's a nice breeze coming upriver from the ocean. The deck is half-filled with customers having an early lunch, but it's such a picturesque Maine summer day that the rest of the tables will fill up quickly. The three elderly amigos are perched in their usual corner, joking over a few iced teas. Every once in a while, their boisterous laughs catch my attention as I go about my tasks and wait on the other patrons. There is nothing out of the ordinary about this day at all. I hope that by the time I'm their age, I will have a few close buddies to pass the time with instead of sitting in my apartment with my dragon.

My mind is preoccupied with two things: a fierce sea dragon and a beautiful woman with whom I have an upcoming date. I feel like a bad movie scene with one of them on either shoulder.

Tiny Valerie is on my left shoulder saying things like, "Oh, Wilder, you're so funny. I'm so glad we finally got to do this," as she strikes a sexy pose and blows me a kiss.

While the mini sea dragon on my right shoulder says, "I will destroy this entire city to find the treasure if I have to."

With a flip of her hair, Valerie winks and coyly tells me, "You're just so handsome and witty. I love hearing about your adventures as a waiter."

Shooting a flame across the front of my face, Draco Marinus threatens, "All of you Protectors will regret the day you ever tried to defeat me."

"I can't remember the last time I had so much fun. This restaurant is just perfect!"

"I'm going to kill you and eat your girlfriend for lunch."

With that imaginary comment, I stumbled as I came back to reality. I had almost dropped the tray of beers I was carrying right into John Patrick's lap, and a stack of cardboard drink coasters went tumbling to the ground.

"Easy there, boy. It'd be a shame to waste a good pint now, wouldn't it?" he laughed as he took the glass from my hand and brought it straight to his lips for a long drink.

"Are you alright, kid?" Red asked. "You were off in dreamland there. Was it a vision?"

"A what?" I looked at him wonderingly. "Is that something that may happen? I've never had visions before."

Jim leaned over the table where they sat outside on the restaurant patio. "Call it a premonition, if you like. Did you see things that could come to pass?"

"Only if that sea dragon turns into an iguana," I joked.

Jim and Red gasped as I bent on one knee to pick up the coasters. John Patrick's eyes were on my chest as he spoke calmly and without emotion, "What? Is? That?"

He raised a finger and pointed at the necklace that had slipped from under my shirt as I bent over and hung down on the front of my chest. I stood back up, coasters in hand, and looked at the men. All three men fixed their gaze on the pendant and old necklace hanging mid-way down my chest. I reached for the pendant, but John Patrick grabbed my hand before I could tuck it back under my shirt.

"Laddie, do ya even know what yer wearing right now?"

The necklace is unremarkable, an old gold chain my grandfather gave me when I turned ten. From the chain hangs a gold pendant. The center is an eye-shaped crystal the size of a quarter, surrounded by intricate gold filagree and carved symbols.

"It's just an old necklace I used to play with at my grandparents' house. Grandpa gave it to me on my tenth birthday. I've worn it since he passed away a few years later." I explained as I gingerly removed John Patrick's hand from my own.

He looked back at his companions and reprised his position at the table. "Can it even be?" he said to Red and Jim. Their faces were still registering the surprise of seeing my old pendant, which confused me to no end. It's just a tacky old piece of jewelry that I thought was cool to play with when I was a kid, and now I wear it in my grandfather's memory.

"There's a reason why you liked to play with the necklace when you were a small boy," Jim began. "You were drawn to the magic it contains and never even knew it. That pendant is an Amulet of Illumination, one of the rarest dragon treasures of all. As far as we know, there have only ever been a handful in existence over the last thousand years."

"Amulet of Illumination? What the heck is that?" I asked as I set the tray on their table and pulled up a chair.

"Hey, Parker, I'm taking a 15!" I looked at the Protectors and waited for a response.

Red was the first to speak. "The Amulet of Illumination allows a user to see hidden objects, regardless of the magic they are concealed by. That includes a dragon in hiding."

I held the amulet in my hands, turning it over and over, touching the carvings and the crystal in the center. I rubbed my thumb over the intricate design, feeling the detailed grooves and intricate flourishes carved into it. I had never imagined it to be anything more than a cool old piece of costume jewelry. It was slightly warm to the touch, and the metal should have felt cool. It was almost soothing to run my thumb over the amulet, feeling the raised pattern and shapes carved into its surface. Although it wasn't large, it held so much detail on its surface that one could imagine even more intricate embellishments within the design that couldn't be seen with the naked eye. The feeling created by looking into the complex and ornate patterns of the amulet was almost hypnotic.

"Wilder," Jim picked up. "That crystal was created by one of the most ancient dragons. They had the power to infuse draconic magic with the very elements of the Earth. It was a way of preserving themselves when they died. In their final moments of life, the ancients could impart some of their magic into their surroundings. One of the most powerful dragons of all was killed in a long-forgotten crystal cavern, and legends say it was able to pass its essence into an exposed crystal in the cavern before it died. The crystal was the purest ever created by nature, and the dragonslayer brought it back to his king. There have been stories that it was split into three pieces, each made into an eye-shaped amulet. The carvings around the crystal serve to not only focus the power, but they also trap the ancient's essence within the amulet."

I glanced at my watch and saw my break was over in another few minutes. The pendant hanging around my neck had taken on a greater weight. Most days, I didn't pay much attention to it, but it felt like an anchor at this moment.

"This Dungeons and Dragons stuff is fun and all, but I need to finish my shift." I noticed a man impatiently waving his empty beer glass in the air. Rudeness will get you nowhere. I'll take my time getting over to his table.

The men started to protest, but I stopped them. "After my shift, I am going home to take Bo for a walk. You're all welcome to join me, and we can talk more then."

With that, I got up and headed to the nearest table to check on my customers. I needed some time to think.

CHAPTER TWENTY

GRANDPA'S GIFT

When I returned to my apartment above the sandwich shop, Bo was ready to get outside. He must have known I was coming because as soon as I opened the door downstairs, he jettisoned to the sidewalk.

"Let's go."

Everyone heard it. At least the other Protectors and I heard it. It seemed so urgent and loud that I wouldn't doubt if Valerie heard it in the store fifty feet away. My stomach let out a little growl of hunger, but I was not sure if that was because I was hungry or my body was trying to trick me into getting a sandwich so that I could see her.

We all headed out for an evening walk in the opposite direction of the store. I didn't want Valerie to catch sight of me passing by the store window without stopping to say hello. She might be offended or ask why there were three old guys walking with me and Bo. Making our way down Main Street, we took up the whole sidewalk on our slow meander past businesses closing up for the day. The sun set a few hours ago, and the moon barely rose in the star-filled sky. That meant no shadows to worry about except those caused by streetlights and passing vehicles.

"Hey, Bo, let's head toward the dog park so you can run around while the guys and I have a little talk," I offered. I hope he takes me up on the suggestion. Sometimes, he gets a bit renegade and has ideas of his own that don't exactly fit with what I need to happen. Tonight was not one of those times, fortunately.

Red seemed lost in thought all the way here from the restaurant. I couldn't tell what was on his mind, but it seemed to be something big and important. John Patrick wasn't his usual self, either. Jim was the only one who seemed normal, but these three always have a way of thinking simpatico, so I'm sure they are all operating on the same wavelength.

"What's on your mind, Red?" I asked. Direct and to the point, that's the best way.

The men seemed to be looking at everything along the sidewalk and road except me, and we walked half a block before Red responded. It appears I'm the only one who wants to be direct this evening.

"Wilder ..." he began. Stopping in his steps, Red turned to me. "We need to talk about that pendant."

I looked at Red, then Jim and John Patrick in turn. They all had grave and concerned expressions on their faces. Jim stepped forward next to Bocephus when a truck passed slowly, blocking the light from creating a shadow on one of the houses along the street. Good thinking.

Jim finally spoke up. "We don't know where your Grandad could have gotten that amulet. But there aren't many people in the world, past or present, that could have had it in their possession. That bit of the puzzle has us a little confused."

Jim took a step forward and looked me in the eye. "Was your Grandad a wizard, son? Did he ever tell you he was skilled in the magic arts?"

I laughed at the thought. "My Grandpa George, a wizard?" He could barely change a light bulb without help. My Grandma always gave him a hard time about taking care of things around their house. If he had been a wizard, he would have been able to handle the basics a bit better."

I never thought much about the necklace he gave me or where it might have come from. It wasn't something that ever came up. "My grandparents lived next door and always encouraged me to tell them stories of the wee folk in the woods, and they encouraged me to share the odd things that happened to me. My parents stifled those parts of my life, but my mom's parents were more accepting. Grandpa had this necklace, which he gave to me on my birthday one year. No big deal."

"On the contrary, laddie," John Patrick said. "It's a very big deal indeed."

By this time, Bo was a few houses further down the street, and we needed to catch up. It's never a good idea to let him get out of sight. Bo is a good dog and a well-behaved dragon, but he doesn't always follow the rules.

I was getting a little concerned regarding the line of commentary and questioning. My grandpa was just my grandpa, no more and no less. They lived in a little house beside us, and I visited them almost daily.

"Let me tell you a story while we walk to the dog park, Wilder," Red said. "I've been in this town for a long time, and I've never met another wizard besides the two gentlemen accompanying us on this walk."

"But for your Grandad to have this amulet," Jim jumped in. "that's mighty surprising, indeed. With the power in that necklace, we won't have to reveal the treasure as bait to bring the sea dragon out. We have the ability to see the little Nessie wherever it's hiding."

I pondered the implications of what the men were suggesting. If my grandpa was a wizard, why would he have kept it from me, considering he would have recognized me as someone with magical abilities, too?

"There's a few other things he gave me over the years ..." I began to share.

At that moment, Bo loudly barked and started running down the street. Twenty feet later, the wings began to sprout. I didn't even know why Bo was starting to go full-on dragon on a residential street. In such moments, I had to remind myself that ordinary people couldn't see a dragon take flight over their homes. By the time Bocephus transformed into Terra Draconis, he would have disappeared to any casual observer. The worst that would happen is someone would wonder, "Where did that little dog vanish to?"

The chase ended as quickly as it had begun, with Bo saying, "Cat. Got away."

We all had a little laugh and continued toward the dog park along the river. There won't be much happening there this time of evening. Oddly enough, Bo likes to interact with other dogs sometimes. Go figure. The dog park is set back two blocks off the main drag, next to a playground. Both overlook the river, so it's a nice place to spend the afternoon while your dog and kids run around in a safe environment. Even after sunset, the parks are a well-lit place for decent folks to hang out, never needing to worry about getting mugged or any shady characters skulking about. There are plenty of other parts of town for them to do their skulking.

Taking a seat on a pair of granite benches along the pathway, we all continued our talk while Bocephus sniffed around the fenced-off dog area as if he were checking messages from other dogs in case someone left an olfactory note for him.

"You mentioned your grandpa gave you a few other curious items over the years," Red began.

"I never said they were curious items," I defended. "Just a couple of junky old things, like his pocket watch I used to play with. It doesn't even work, but I didn't have the heart to throw it away. It never even kept time when I was little. I always figured that was why Grampa didn't care if I played with it."

I pulled the round gold watch out of my front pocket and popped open the cover to expose the clock face. "See?" I said, offering it to Jim. "Just an old pocket watch that isn't even right twice a day."

I dangled the watch on its tarnished gold chain and watched it twinkle in the light from the streetlights. Then, an odd thing happened. The watch didn't precisely dangle properly on the chain. Under the customary laws of gravity, the watch would hang straight down to the ground from the point of suspension. This watch, however, had a decidedly noticeable lean to it in the direction of the three men sitting across from m e.

"Do you guys see what's happening here?" I asked. "Am I imagining this?"

"Have ye put a charm on that wee timepiece?" John Patrick asked quietly and curiously.

I hadn't, and I told them so. "What kind of charm would I put on an old broken pocket watch? I carry it for good luck because it reminds me of my grandpa."

I stood up and walked away from the bench. The further I walked, the more of a sideways angle the pocket watch had on the chain. I stepped in a half-circle around the other Protectors, and the watch kept pointing at them, as true as a compass pointing north.

"It's charmed!" Red said as he jumped up from the bench. "It tracks us."

Jim eyed the watch warily and spoke next, "The boy had never heard of Protectors until a short time ago, but somehow, this watch in his possession is able to point us out."

Continuing my walk and watching the pocket watch do its work, I offered a thought. "Like a tracking spell?" I asked. "Someone put a charm on this pocket watch to swing around and help find a Protector or other wizard?"

Bo came running toward us and leaped over the dog area chain-link fence in a quick bound that his breed shouldn't have been capable of. Stopping a few feet short of where I was standing, he sniffed the air toward the watch as it still leaned toward Red.

"Spell for finding wizards. Very old," Bo told us.

Dragons know things. If Bo is typical of dragons, he sometimes knows things but doesn't offer any explanation of how. This is one of those moments.

"Very old magic," he repeated as he walked to the nearest tree to take a leak.

Red walked back a few steps to the granite bench and sighed as he sat. The weariness of his thoughts showed on his face in the glow of the streetlights. "Wilder, you may want to pull up a bench. I have a tale to tell you. I think I know where your grandfather got those items, and the answer is going to change your world."

"In every heart, there is a dragon yearning to be free."

C.S. Lewis

CHAPTER TWENTY-ONE

GROWING CONFIDENCE

We've spent a lot of time around the table throwing out ideas about where the sea dragon is hiding and how the dragons got here in the first place. Nobody has offered any ideas that have any good roots. It's all a guessing game, but we know we need to avoid a dragon battle at all costs. They want their treasure, and they want to destroy each other. It's hard to believe my little drooling furball is a centuries-old dragon resolute on the demise of his nemesis.

Bocephus likes being here because of the tasty snacks and is willing to work with us to trick the other dragon into returning to where it came from. I'm not sure I totally understand where that is. The Protectors keep referring to "the other side" and "beyond the veil." I do know the other side doesn't have Twinkies or cats, so Bo is happy to help us.

A cool breeze flowed from the ocean, down the river's mouth and into the city as the sun warmed the streets. In these early dawn hours, I like to grab a coffee from the diner down the street, sit in the park, and watch the water flow past as I collect my thoughts for the day. I was never so introspective before this dragon development, but now I wonder if I've been squandering my abilities on inconsequential things instead of making a difference. The other side of my brain says I have been making a difference, only in more minor, less noticeable ways.

I thought about that kid I saved last winter from being hit by a garbage truck by blowing out the truck tire, and the grandma back in the spring who would have had years of painful skin grafts if I hadn't rerouted that spilled hot coffee at the restaurant. I surprised myself at the level of power I had at my disposal one day when I saw a paraglider falling from the sky at the beach last summer. The paraglider must have gotten caught in a downdraft because it suddenly plummeted from a hundred feet above the sand, headed directly to an oblivious couple walking hand-in-hand down the beach. There indeed would have been serious injuries if I hadn't redirected the paraglider and controlled its descent, even lifting it back up to a level flight again. It had been merely a dozen feet above their heads when I saw it. The paraglider must have told stories of their awesomeness and exceptional recovery skills afterward.

I make a difference and don't need to convince myself. There's so much more I can do. I can see it now.

CHAPTER TWENTY-TWO

RESCUE AT SEA

Maine is a popular vacation spot. The coastline goes from beautiful sandy beaches to a jagged rocky shore and back to beaches again. There are lakes and mountains and the beauty of pristine nature everywhere you look. Tourists tend to do things they would never do at home on an ordinary day, often getting them into trouble. That's precisely what happened to a trio of kids in a small sailboat.

Me and Bo were hanging out in my apartment on a beautiful sunny Saturday afternoon. I had just spent the entire brunch shift working outside on the tavern patio, so I had my fill of fresh air for the day. Give me a Shipyard Export Ale and a good movie, and we'll be happy for the afternoon. I was just about to turn off the radio when the DJ said three kids were missing in a Sunfish sailboat off the coast somewhere between Peaks Island and Halfway Rock Lighthouse. A thick bank of fog had rolled in, and the kids might have been lost in it.

I know the kind of sailboat they are in from back in my summer camp days. There's no radio or shelter for the three ten-year-old boys who left their camp on Peaks Island this morning. The fog has dropped visibility to mere feet, and where they were last spotted can be a busy area for larger vessels and fishing boats.

"Bo, we need to head out," I said as I grabbed my long wool coat to ward off the ocean chill. I've become accustomed to wearing it on our night flights.

"How do you feel about a little flight over the ocean?"

He chuffed, "As long as we can watch the movie when we get back."

My tv-addicted dog never fails to let his opinion be known. Being a dragon hundreds of years old gives him every right to speak up.

I went to the marine channel using the scanner app on my phone. I've been relying on that a lot lately, listening for any calls that might be a sign of the sea dragon causing trouble. The harbor master said the search party is waiting for the fog to let up, and the Coast Guard doesn't have any boats or equipment that can offer much assistance until that time, either.

No help, no search parties, no radio, no cell phones. That leaves magic to seek out the kids and get them to safety. Even though I learn a bit more daily from my three new mentors, I'm still not a wizard who uses spells. I can accomplish the same magic with intention. I only need to have a clear vision in my mind of what I want to happen. If I'm strong enough, reality bends to my will. So far, so good. I can feel when something I want to accomplish seems like it's too much for my magic to handle, so I usually rethink the idea and quickly come up with a different option. I haven't ever tried moving or lifting anything heavy like a dump truck that's about to run over a puppy, but with Bo's help and energy, I feel more capable than ever.

Minutes later, we're in the air, passing over the pier at Old Orchard Beach and heading northeast toward the islands of Casco Bay. There are over 300 islands in the bay, but we're concentrating our search in the vicinity of the camp on Peaks Island from which they sailed this morning. Bo flew fast, and even at this altitude, I could taste the briny air as the wind whipped against my face. I had learned quickly to wear ski goggles whenever we flew. I must look like one of those old World War One aviators from the open-cockpit biplanes, but nobody can see me anyway. Magical invisibility has many advantages.

I try not to feel too confident, but we have an advantage in our search that nobody else has. At this point, I think we're the only ones searching for the kids, anyway. Everyone else is praying for a positive outcome. I hope we can be the answer to their prayers, even though they'll never know how the rescue happened, as long as we do it right. Anonymity is key. We can't have any newspaper headlines about a flying dragon with a goofy goggle-eyed man on its back ushering the kids to safety in their tiny sailboat.

As we approached Portland Head Light on our left, the fog that socked in the entire bay got even thicker. The world-famous eighty-foot tall gleaming white lighthouse with the red-roofed lighthouse keeper cottage next to it was hardly visible, the beam from the tower barely piercing the dense fog. The air feels cool and damp, and I kept wiping a finger across my goggles to clear the water droplets that accumulated. The air was heavy with moisture, and every sound from below was muffled. Once out in the worst of it, there's no way sound could even carry more than a few hundred feet if the boys yell for help.

"Okay, buddy. Let's get closer to the water, and I hope we find these kids before something bad happens."

"I can see a lot better than you," Bo reminded me. "Close your eyes and use my dragon sight."

Dragons can see in many visual wavelengths and spectrums that human eyes aren't capable of seeing. Closing my eyes and reaching out with my mind, I tapped into Bo's mind to see what he can see. The vision change was stunning, causing my brain to misfire for a minute until I could bring it under control. The assault of light and color caught me off-guard, even though I expected it to be different from my regular sight.

The fog was still visible, but I could see through it more clearly. The dense fog no longer obscured boats in the bay below. Islands in the distance that were completely shrouded moments before popped clearly into view. The colors of every object in my range of vision were magnified, with shades and hues I had never seen before. If Bo's vision looked like this in the thick fog, I can't even imagine what he sees on a sunny day.

"Lower," he warned as we dropped closer to the water. A dragon of few words.

The sea was calm, much more so than usual. There was hardly a ripple in the ocean. Not a wave or splash to be seen or heard. The pure silence in the blanket of fog was as predominant as if I were wearing noise-canceling headphones. The only sound was the mighty whoosh of Bo's wings as we flew low over the water, alert for any sign of the missing trio.

Reaching out with magic, I searched for the boys using my mind and powers. Thanks to our newly found connection, Bo augmented my abilities, making us an effective search-and-rescue team. We searched for what seemed like hours, covering many square miles of the bay, island to island, with no luck. Our magic felt stifled in a way that I can't even explain. I should be able to detect them better than this. I've never tried a search for missing people, but I expected to have better results. As we passed near Cliff Island, the outermost island in the harbor, I felt the sensation I had been waiting for.

"Bank to the right," I asked. "There's something there."

"I see them," Bo alerted me. "I see the little sailboat."

There was no wind at all in this fog and no motion of the ocean below. Their small sailboat was trapped in the middle of Casco Bay, miles from any land. These boys had no hope of getting home safely anytime soon unless this weird weather let up. The fog felt unnatural, but I'm not sure why.

We swooped low toward the kids. I could see their faces, frightened but brave, each keeping a calm exterior to not alarm the others. Bo knew what he had to do while I did the wizard thing. Hovering in mid-air, Bo pressed his magnificent leathery wings against the dense, thick white fog. A breeze began to stir, gentle at first, then intensifying.

As the sail on the tiny boat fluttered and filled with air, I directed my energy toward the water around the boat. Pushing my will to the surface, I created a moving channel of water, flowing toward the distant island shore and allowing the watercraft to move in the current.

"We're moving, we're moving!" one of the boys shouted, as they all begin to cheer.

Their whooping and hollering cut through the fog like a hot knife through butter, lodging deep in my heart with satisfaction.

As we flew in a circle around the tiny boat, I kept my focus on the narrow canal of current carrying the boys back home. Twenty minutes later, they bumped into the dock they had left from hours before. My homing spell had done its trick.

"They say dragons never truly die. No matter how many times you kill them."
S.G. Rogers, Jon Hansen and the Dragon Clan of Yden

Chapter Twenty-Three

THE HIDDEN CAVE

Brunch on Sunday can be a busy time at Red's Riverside Tavern. Two-for-one mimosa specials tend to bring in a lot of people. Even though the day was a bit cool to start, the tables were primarily full inside and out as I made my way around, attentively refilling bottomless cups of coffee and taking orders for scrambled eggs and hash browns. It was pure luck the group of amateur ghosthunters sat in my section before the big ghost hunt they had planned for the rest of the day.

"Nobody has ever ordered pancakes for an entire table before," I said with a chuckle. "Are you sure all 6 of you want pancakes? We have amazing chicken and waffles."

The tall, lanky dude at the end of the table explained, "We're the Maine Haunt Hunters. It's tradition to have a big pancake breakfast before a ghost hunt."

Without waiting for me to ask another question, he went on. "It's not the fake kind of thing you see on TV, either. We're for real, and we've found quite a few ghosts in haunted buildings around the area. We have a YouTube channel with lots of videos."

The blue-haired girl across the table was excited when she interjected, "Today we're going in the caverns under the mills across the river." She pointed across the outdoor deck toward the other side of the Saco River. "There are a hundred years' worth of stories, local legends, and so many rumors of hauntings in those factories. Lots of families lost their loved ones in mill accidents over the years, and their spirits may still be there."

"Not a place most people can usually go, I guess?" I asked politely, making conversations and hoping for good tips. This crew looked like they'd be scrounging for enough to cover breakfast, so I didn't have any high hopes for more than ten percent.

Blue-hair was excited when she answered, "They finally permitted us to go under the factory. The water in the cavern was originally used as some sort of cooling system for the steam engines in the old mills. Lots of people died there over the years."

"There's even rumors of secret underground tunnels that come out under the river," said the chubby guy wearing a tuxedo t-shirt and top hat at the far end of the table. "That's how the water gets into the cavern. It's so cool, and I can't wait to see it!" Tuxedo awkwardly high-fived the tall pancake-ordering dude.

I looked out from the dining patio perspective at the scene across the river. The massive five-story brick factory sat 50 feet above the water line. The brick smokestacks reached high into the sky, easily a hundred feet above the rooftops. The building foundations were supported by a steep stone wall that rose from the water's surface. I had never imagined there could be a cave under there, let alone one that possibly has water access. I should have paid more attention to local history. If a cave has a passage to the river, especially if the passage is filled with water, that would be a perfect hiding place for a water dragon. It was too perfect, too secretive. If the cave had a hidden entrance big enough for a dragon to enter and exit, it would be the ideal hiding place.

"Draco Marinus," I whispered to myself as I gently shoved Lanky Pancake Dude aside and sat on the bench beside him. "Tell me more about this, please. There's a cavern under the mill right over there?" I pointed over the river to the factory with its tall smokestack silhouetted against the brightening midday sun. Lanky Dude shifted in his new seat and answered, "We heard it's wicked cool. Do you want to come with us? We're always looking for new members. We're heading over there after the pancakes." He shrugged, "But you're probably still working."

"My shift ends when your pancakes are ready," I said quickly. "I just have to run home and get something first."

The river was once the region's lifeblood, its flow constant and deep. It swept everything in its path, but if you knew how to navigate it, it could also hide you from the world. With its serpentine body and aquatic prowess, a water dragon could slip into such a passage unnoticed, using the river to hide and travel. If the cave had access to the river—if that passage flooded even just a little—it would be an almost perfect sanctuary.

Perfect for a creature that thrived in the murky depths and elusive currents.

I could almost picture it now: the dragon coiled within the dark, damp confines of the cave, its gleaming scales reflecting even the faintest traces of light. The sound of the river rushing outside, muffled but constant, blended with the creature's steady breathing. It would be a haven where no one could reach it, and no one could disturb its peace. A place where Draco Marinus could vanish as effortlessly as it had arrived, leaving only ripples in the water as its trace.

But was it possible? Could there be such a passage? The idea made my pulse quicken. The implications were enormous if the cave truly existed, hidden beneath that massive stone wall. I had to find out. If the ancient legendary water dragon was indeed living there and had been hiding in plain sight all these weeks, I had just stumbled across something far more significant than I had imagined.

The thought made my stomach knot with excitement and fear. So many questions came to mind. This could be a grave danger for the intrepid team of ghost hunters that sat at the table with me. Would the dragon be hostile? Would it even care about them, or would they be something to be simply destroyed and never seen again?

I swallowed hard, steeling myself for what I knew I must do. I needed to go with them as the group's Protector. If the cave was real and connected to the river in the way I imagined, I had to see it for myself.

PACKING FOR BATTLE

I tried to think quickly in my apartment as I started tossing supplies into my backpack.

"Bo," I said with some trepidation, knowing how he was about to react. "I think I know where DM is."

Jumping on the back of the couch to be face-level with me, Bo demanded, "Tell me now, and I will kill it." He was very insistent and confident. I could feel the power of his will pressing at me, urging me to tell him where the sea dragon was hiding.

"Stop doing that. We're going together. And there will be a few other people that might need our help and protection."

"Don't care," Bo said, jumping down and pacing the floor. His claws were clicking more than usual. I looked and saw they had grown impossibly large, and he was fifty percent bigger than usual. My little bulldog was now the size of a German Shepherd.

I needed to calm him down before things got out of control. "Hold on, buddy. You can't go into dragon mode in the apartment. Slow down and be patient. We can't lose this opportunity."

I also didn't want a giant Bocephus-shaped hole knocked through my wall if he decided to fly off without me, and without going outside first. Even worse, I'm sure his full size would blow the roof off this building, and his weight would undoubtedly collapse the floor.

I filled him in on the stories the ghost gang had told me – of the hauntings, the deaths, and most importantly, the secret water-filled tunnel from the river to the cavern under the old mills.

"Hurry," he panted. "Must hurry. The water dragon is angry and desperate and doesn't care who lives or dies. It only wants the treasure."

"And you," I finished. "It wants to kill you." A black pit formed in my gut as I said the words out loud. This dog has become such a massive part of my life I can't even imagine losing him now. The emotional dragon/rider connection was also unmistakable. We were beginning to feel what each other felt, and we've often been having conversations without even speaking aloud. It's new for both of us. Even though Bo has lived for centuries, he said he's never had a connection with a human before.

I grabbed my necklace through my t-shirt to ensure the Amulet of Illumination was there. I rarely took it off except for a shower or bedtime, but this wasn't the time to leave anything to chance. A sudden thought came to mind, and I tested the crystal.

Holding it up to my eye, I looked in Bo's direction. There was no dog visible through the amulet. My entire field of vision was taken up by a wall of shimmering red scales, reflecting the light from the end table and the TV on the other side of the room. Bo's true image filled the entire room, floor to ceiling, and I stood there dumbfounded at the sight.

"What are you doing?" he said with a lot of tone in his deep dragon voice. "We've got shit to kill and ghost hunters to protect. Stop staring into that thing, and let's go."

I need to tell him about the amulet so he understands its importance.

"I know about the crystal," Bo responded to my unspoken thought. Okay, that was weird and will take a lot of getting used to.

He continued, giving me even more details about the story we didn't already know. "I can feel the energy of his life hanging from your neck. Very powerful."

"What? How long have you known?"

"Always," Bo said. "Always. I felt the presence of the ancient from the moment we first met. Even though that dragon lived and died millennia before me, we are still all connected in the power of the Earth. Saint George collected the crystal when he slayed the monstrous beast and the greatest of all dragon legends was born."

"Saint George?" I asked. That is one of the oldest and most re-told dragon stories of all time. It's an important story in the Catholic religion. In the 11th century, a mighty dragon terrorized a village, demanding daily tribute. Eventually, the villagers were forced to resort to human sacrifices. The legend of Saint George defeating that dragon is a famous tale in Christianity, perhaps as an example of light conquering darkness.

"You're telling me that story is true, and I'm wearing a crystal formed when Saint George – THE Saint George, the most famous dragonslayer of all time – defeated the dragon and saved a princess?"

"Slaying dragons isn't something I usually like to talk about," Bo said slowly, his eyes glowing. "But yes, the story is true, and the amulet hangs around your neck. I can feel what is left of the dragon inside of it. When are we leaving?"

Bo's impatience showed as he circled the couch, then the kitchen table, then the recliner, then the door, and back to the couch again.

"Don't forget your sword," Bo shouted on one of his trips into the kitchen and back. "You should bring the sword to slay the water dragon."

I laughed at the image of me brandishing a sword, like a medieval knight riding into battle.

"Sounds like I would probably hurt myself," I said. "Plus, I don't own a sword, so there's that little problem with your plan."

"You are so blind." Bo stared at me unblinkingly, waiting for me to understand.

"I don't understand."

"Can't you feel it here in your apartment? All of your Protector friends missed it, too."

I would need a little help if we were ever going to get out of the apartment in time to join Blue Hair, Lanky Pancake Dude, and Tuxedo Guy on their ghost hunt.

"I will help," Bo offered.

I felt the tendrils of power flowing from him, joining with my own energies and creating a new flow of sensations, unlocking awareness I hadn't felt before.

"In the closet. There's something in the closet very powerful," I said. "But it's hidden from detection. I never noticed it before, but we can sense it together."

"Powerful spells can conceal ancient objects of power."

I walked the short distance across the living room floor, feeling the power of whatever was in the hall closet strengthen with each step. This new arrangement was opening up a lot of new perceptions for me.

"Is a glow coming from under the closet door, or am I imagining it?"

Bo chuffed, "Just open the door and get the sword. We need to leave."

"I don't own a sword," I reiterated as I opened the closet door.

"Holy crap, I own a sword."

The gleaming metal sword is a little over three feet long, resting on the right side of the open closet next to a broom and my umbrella. It glows slightly in the semi-darkness of the closet, unmistakable in its specialness. The blade is patterned in mysterious and intricate fine markings, like frosty whorls left on a car hood on a cold winter morning. It's 3 inches wide at the hilt and tapered to a wicked point at the floor. The metal pommel, covered in Romanesque scrollwork, terminates on each end with a cross centered inside a golden orb. The handle of ancient wood is wrapped in red leather, and it felt warm and powerful under my fingertips as I began to lift it from the closet.

"Where did this come from? I've never seen this before in my life," I mused aloud to myself. But it was Bocephus who answered.

"Close your eyes and look at the sword."

"Those instructions are a little confusing, but okay."

I closed my eyes and held the sword in front of me. Almost as if a portal opened up in my forehead, a pinhole swirled open to a dime size, then a quarter. Within a few seconds, I saw with a wizard's sight, using my mind's eye like a hotel door peephole into the world. It's another mythical thing I've only read about and never believed to be true.

"This is my grandpa's walking stick," I said quietly. "Grandma gave this to me right after he died, along with the amulet and a few other things."

"Are you done yet? I have a dragon to kill."

That's my Bo, always keeping me on task. He's right, though. Those ghost hunters won't wait forever, and I can't have them heading into danger without me there to protect them.

With the sword in my hand, we headed down the stairs to the door. It's obviously disguised with a potent concealment spell that has lasted for a long time. I can't take the time now to try and figure this out, but maybe the guys will have some insight about Grandpa George and his magical walking stick.

"The dragon's lair is where courage is tested and legends are born."

J.R.R. Tolkien

Chapter Twenty-Five

WHO YOU GONNA CALL?

Thankfully, the ghost-hunting club was still waiting for me when I returned to the restaurant. I had asked Parker to make bottomless pancakes for them on my way out, and he must have complied.

"We don't offer that on the menu," he said quizzically when I mentioned it.

"I just need you to please do this favor for me and not ask questions. I'll pay for it out of my tips if you want."

"No need," Parker looked at me. "If it's important to you for any reason, I'm happy to help out. It's kind of weird, but whatever you need is fine with me!"

Fast-forward twenty minutes, and Chubby Tuxedo Boy was mopping up the last of the syrup on his plate as I slid into an empty seat at the end of the table. The others looked jacked up on coffee and ready to jump out of their skins. It would be interesting to see if they find anything even remotely ghostly.

"You're back!" Blue Hair said with a smile. "Does that mean we're ready to go? We already paid the check."

There's a pedestrian bridge across the river from the restaurant parking lot to a walking path through the old mills on the other side. There are a bunch of apartments, businesses, and breweries on the other side, so it's good to keep customer access open. As we crossed the two-hundred-foot suspension bridge across the river, I realized how vulnerable we would be if Draco Marinus suddenly appeared in the water below us.

"We have to meet the security guard at the back entrance," Lanky Pancake Dude said. "I texted him when we left the restaurant, so he knows we're on the way."

A gust of wind from upriver took off Chubby Tuxedo Boy's top hat, but Bo saved the day by jumping up and grabbing it between his teeth. That was a big surprise to everyone since Bo is the closest to the ground and doesn't look like the type of dog that can do any sort of tricks.

"Great trick!" Blue Hair girl said as she clapped her hands. "How'd you teach him to do that?"

"Oh, Bocephus is just full of surprises," I quipped. That's an understatement if there ever was one. Bo looked up at me as if he was about to say something but thought better of it.

Once we arrived at the security entrance, the guard began to walk us down a labyrinthine path of hallways, stairs, and over-sized sliding metal doors that had been in place for a century or more. At first, the hallways were public areas with doors to various businesses on either side. Still, after a few turns and flights of stairs, we walked into an older part of the factory that wasn't normally accessible.

As if he knew what I was wondering, the guard offered, "These big doors served as fire breaks between sections of the old mill buildings." Unfortunately, they also occasionally prevented workers from being able to escape when they needed to. One fire killed over 50 workers when they couldn't get the door open. The intense heat of the fire melted the rollers in their tracks. They've been upgraded since, but it was a bad day in the history of this old factory."

"You've probably heard a lot of stories about these buildings," Lanky Pancake Dude pressed. "Anything you're willing to share with us?"

The guard looked at each of us, eye to eye, slowly sizing us up as if deciding how much information we could handle.

"Nope."

That was a big disappointment. Blue Hair sighed as if she had been holding her breath in anticipation of some great stories from the security guard.

"Anything special we should know before we get to the cooling cavern?" She was trying a different angle. Great idea.

We had already descended a few flights, and he didn't slow his pace down the metal stairs as the guard responded, "I'm not a big believer in ghosts, but you kids have permission to check out the cavern under the factory building, so I'm taking you there. Our director seems to be a big fan of your YouTube channel, so you get special access to an area visitors usually don't get access to. It's pretty cool down there, but be careful. The security cameras have been shorting out a lot lately, so we don't always have a real-time view of the area."

That odd development piqued my curiosity. "Do you often have trouble with the security cameras? Are they just old and wonky?"

"Not at all," the guard said. "We've got modern, hi-tech cameras down there and in all the important areas of the building. There are a lot of condos and apartments on the upper floors, and businesses pay good money to be in these amazing old buildings. The owners are committed to safety and security. That's why I'm here, so if you kids have another agenda ..."

"No other agenda," Blue Hair jumped in. "We are here for exactly what we told you." She hooked her thumbs left and right at her friends, "We're the Maine Haunt Hunters, and we're looking for ghosts."

"Good luck with that," he said as we stopped at a large metal door crisscrossed with reinforced steel bands. "We're here."

With an ear-piercing metallic scraping sound, the guard slid open the heavy metal door to reveal the cavern beyond. The view from a catwalk looked down twenty feet to the rocky surface, with the unmistakable glistening of water only a few dozen feet from the cavern wall.

"There's lights!" Blue Hair said with surprise. "I didn't expect there to be electricity."

"You can't have security cameras without electricity," the guard laughed. "Some of the lighting is original from back a hundred years ago. We don't use those for fear of an electrical short. Those don't illuminate very well, anyway. Back in the fifties, they installed these light trusses, which you can see overhead. Those beams hold better lighting in case anyone ever needs to see shit down here. Excuse my French."

We all began to descend the grated metal stairs, holding tightly to the railing bolted directly onto the cavern wall.

The guard went on as if he were giving a guided tour, "I'm sure you've heard all the stories, but these caverns were here long before the factory was built overhead. The old-timers could pump up the cold water from here to cool off the mill equipment, and then it would drain back down and out into the river. It was probably as polluted as hell, but nobody cared back then. Excuse my French again. There are a few places where the river water enters the cavern via an underground side current. Stay away from anything that looks like moving water. That's not a safe area to be, and it's not exactly easy to get a paramedic down here."

That was the kind of story I wanted to hear. Now, I just needed to shake the guard and kids so I could take a look around the cavern with the Amulet of Illumination.

Bo and I started to wander a bit as the Maine Haunt Hunters set up their ghost-monitoring equipment. They had an EMF proximity detector that would register spirits nearby, a ghost box to hear if a ghost wanted to communicate, and a bunch of microphones set up around the floor for recording EVPs of ghost noises. These kids had some good tech, just like the gear I usually see on the ghost-hunting TV shows. I was impressed.

Bo nudged my leg as I was trying to raise the amulet to my eye unobtrusively. "I can smell it. It's been here but is gone now." He continued to sniff at the damp cavern air, drawing in huge nostrils full of the scent of his mortal enemy.

"Are you sure?" I wanted to know. "I mean, are you sure it's been here?"

"I can smell it. The entire cavern reeks of Draco Marinus. Like old fish and burned-out ships and thousands of dead sailors."

"How do you really feel?" I joked.

"Not here now," Bo said as he lifted his leg and almost peed on me.

"You did that on purpose," I hissed at him.

"Don't know what you mean," he chuffed as he wandered off to sniff more areas of the cavern.

Although surprisingly well-lit, the cavern was still replete with dark areas. The jagged rock ceiling above the light trusses was barely visible in some of the darker areas, but there wasn't enough room for a dragon to hide up there. Draco Marinus would more likely be in the large pool of black water in the middle of the cavern, hiding and waiting to attack.

The water was still, not a ripple disturbing the surface. The ghosters had spent an hour with their equipment asking questions aloud, hoping for a response from the other side.

"We'll check the recording later for any EVPs," Blue Hair shouted up to the guard. "I think our hour is just about up."

As they began the task of clean-up and packing away their rather expensive electronics, Bo and I made one last trip around the edge of the cooling pond, long out of use but still accessible.

"I wonder what makes the cameras malfunction," I asked Bo. "Do you think the proximity of magic causes that?"

"I don't have any problem watching your TV while you are at work, so that's not it. Dragons are very powerful, and a cloaking spell may short out the cameras. They can't operate. When the cameras go out, the dragon is probably here in the cavern but cloaked to stay invisible and remain out of sight."

We had found the answers we came looking for. Now, we need to tell the other Protectors about the dragon and the cavern and set our plan into motion before it finds the Protector's hidden treasure.

CHAPTER TWENTY-SIX

DOWN BELOW

"There's no way that plan will work," I had said to the other Protectors. "You can't just wave your hand at the security guard and expect him to guide us to the cavern without permission or authorization to access the area."

"Nae, you shouldn't be so dootsome," John Patrick tutted at me, stomping his wooden walking stick on the floor for emphasis. "You'll be surprised in this life where a wee bit of confidence and a tottie of magic can get you."

Sure enough, as we approached the security gate I had entered with the ghost hunters, the guard stood up from his small desk and walked out, looking at me when he said, "Nobody told me you were coming back. This is unexpected. The kids weren't good enough, so you had to come back with a few more experienced men?" he chortled as he hiked up his big belt with both hands. "I can't let you in, sorry."

Jim stepped before the man, eyeballing him from two feet away. The move caused the guard to flinch a bit before he regained his composure. After all, he was a building security guard, and this wasn't a high-level secure zone or military operation—just an office building keeping safety a priority.

"You're mistaken," Jim said quietly, with a slight tilt of his head and a small hand gesture. "You can let us in after all. You'll take us to the cavern right away."

The guard blinked back at Jim. Then he smiled and responded perfectly naturally and unaffectedly, "Oh, hold on, I made an error. I'll take you all down to the cavern right away. Sorry about that misunderstanding, fellas."

My eyes must have almost bugged out of my head because Jim and Red both saw my reaction and laughed.

"Just a little enchantment spell," Jim explained to me. "Nothing to be concerned about, no side-effects other than memory loss of the next few hours. He'll just think he fell asleep at his desk or something."

John Patrick carried a walking stick that barely ever touched the ground, Red had an umbrella in his hand as if he expected it to rain at any moment, and Jim was holding a long flashlight, the only sensible thing between the three of them. In my left hand I tapped Grandpa's walking stick on the ground. I could clearly see it was a sword, but to everyone else, it was only a carved stick.

"Let's get moving. We have a lot of ground to cover," I asserted.

As the guard led us down the first hallway, Red stopped and used the handle of his umbrella to tap on a door that looked different than the others. "I heard there are a lot of stairs. Can we just take the elevator?"

I laughed at his question since it seemed so absurd after my multi-flight walk down a bunch of rickety old iron stairs yesterday. He immediately side-eyed me, so my laugh was cut short.

"Of course," the guard said back to Red. "Let me hit that panel next to you with my keycard, and we can take the elevator down to one floor above the cavern." He opened the door to reveal an old elevator that looked like it hadn't been used much for the last few decades.

"What?" I gaped at Red, then the guard. I must have looked like a cartoon character, whipping my head back and forth multiple times. "Wait, what?"

"You don't know until you ask, kiddo," John Patrick said with a chuckle. Pile in, laddies. Dogs and old men first."

The elevator was far from modern. It reminded me of something you might have seen in an old movie with a manual metal gate instead of sliding doors. The guard slid the gate closed again after we all got in, and the elevator began its slow, jerky descent to the cavern a few flights below. When the door opened, we were right down the hall from the big metal door that marked the entrance to the cooling cavern. I was still shaking my head in disbelief when we got to the metal-banded security door.

"Why didn't you bring the ghost hunters down here on the elevator yesterday?" I directed at the mesmerized guard.

His answer was quick and honest, "I gave them the full experience. They needed to feel like this was a mysterious and hidden location, difficult to find and even rarer to gain entry."

"Right," I continued. "Not just a quick Great Gatsby elevator ride down a few flights. The only thing missing was an old elevator operator smoking a stogie."

We were all gathered in front of the final door. Beyond this point, it is possible we may encounter a fight with a dragon we've only heard stories about. The veracity of those stories remains to be seen, but there are plenty of other legendary tales I've learned that are true in the last few months.

"Let's get moving," Bo barked gruffly. "I have killing to do."

Non-plussed at the talking dog, the security guard deftly opened the big door, giving us all a view of the cavern beyond and below. Jim turned to the guard and suggested he return to his office.

"I think I'll head back to my office now, fellas. Holler if you need anything." He turned and departed, closing the heavy metal door behind himself.

Bo was the first to descend into the cavern, bounding down the metal stairs two at a time until he was sniffing the ground below only seconds later. The Protectors were more careful and deliberate. Even though their lives have been centuries long, they don't want any unnecessary injuries or broken bones causing a problem today.

Red, the first to reach the bottom, ambled across the cavern floor to the water's edge. There was no movement, not even a ripple on the surface. A moment later, John Patrick and Jim were by his side. The magic in the air was palpable to me, their incredible resources and talents in full use. The Protectors were "feeling" for Draco Marinus, a task they had been waiting for centuries to begin. The cavern was silent, except for Bo's sniffing across the rocks and around the old equipment rusting away near the massive underground lagoon.

"Laddie, time to bring out that crystal of yours," John Patrick urged. "Have a look around the place and tell us what you see."

Placing the Amulet of Illumination to my right eye, the dark cavern blossomed into a well-lit area. Nothing would be capable of hiding from my view using this crystal, especially a dragon. The three men looked relatively normal to my sight, although their entire bodies emitted an unnatural glow. Their powers were even detectable with this amulet, I registered. As I turned for a look across the lagoon, my field of vision passed where Bocephus had been waiting. My eyes were momentarily blinded by the assault of crimson light beaming from his tiny body. Although he was in dog form, the crystal showed me his true dragon body in full splendor. There were so many shades of brilliant color: crimson, burgundy, scarlet, and every possible hue of red emanating from his body and wings.

"Wow," I spoke aloud. "Magic is so freaking cool."

Although my grandfather had kept this amulet's true purpose hidden from me, it clearly worked for me today. Shifting my gaze to the lagoon, I saw a slight glow coming from deep under the water's surface. This wasn't light reflecting off the water from the trusses overhead. It seemed a bit odd, so I began to mention it to the men standing on the rocks at the water's edge. Before I could get the first words out of my mouth, the light grew brighter and seemed closer to the surface.

"Get away from the lagoon!" I shouted at them suddenly. "Get back now!"

Instead, the three Protectors stood their ground, each drawing a hidden weapon and preparing their stance for a fight. The walking stick, umbrella, and flashlight were transformed into fierce-looking swords, their concealment by magic no longer needed. What I now saw through the amulet was three strong and capable fighters, knights of old ready to do battle once again.

Bo had heard me shout my warning, and he was already transforming when the sea dragon burst through the surface. One mighty flap of his powerful wings took him to the top of a nearby old pumping station, the mighty dragon perched atop the ancient rusting hulk of equipment. The element of surprise lost; the fight would now begin in earnest. More than a dozen feet of sinewy, heavily muscled, scaly Draco Marinus wavered above the water, its head keeping Bo and the Protectors well within sight.

"I know you," the sea dragon spoke slowly. The voice sounded as though it came from underwater, thick and wet and unnatural sounding. "I know you all. I will never forget the smell of an enemy, especially one that is not easily vanquished. Even more so one who escaped me."

The hiss in the sea dragon's speech was unsettling, with long, airy ess sounds spoken in a whisper. It created a feeling of unease that chilled me to the bone. More and more of the beast rose to the surface, forming a protective coil around the neck and head, now held proudly fifteen feet above the water. The green scales were iridescent and shining in the light from the trusses above, the myriad shades of green reflecting the meager light. I realized I no longer needed the Amulet of Illumination to see the dragon. It had given up on a cloaking spell and floated arrogantly and unconcealed on the water in front of us.

"Since The Protectors banished us from this world ages ago, I have waited for my chance to return and seek out the treasure stolen from me and my kin. It is a welcome bonus that I will also defeat the one other remaining dragon. Terra Draconis, today will be your final day on this planet. Prepare to meet your ancestors."

It seemed impossible that I was seeing this sea dragon floating on the surface of the black lagoon in this underground cavern in our small Maine town. Things like this don't happen here. Things like this don't really happen anywhere, do they?

The sea dragon slowly shifted his gaze and directed his attention at John Patrick. "I remember you, wizard. You may have escaped me once, but you do not travel with a snake's head today. You were lucky in our last meeting so long ago, but today will mark the end of you."

"You!" John Patrick exclaimed. "You were the Beithir I fought in Scotland five hundred years ago. Aye, I escaped with my life that day, something you will not do today." He stood proudly with his gleaming sword gripped tightly in both hands as a challenge to the menace in front of him.

Since no explanation was forthcoming, I had to ask, "Can someone please explain this to me? You guys have battled before?"

Red was the first one to give me a response, "A Beithir is a dragon in Scottish folklore, but now you know it is very, very real. The Beithir has a deadly venomous sting, and the only cure is made from water in which the head of another snake has been placed, or to reach the nearest loch or river before the dragon does. Those are the only ways to survive, and John Patrick did so, many years ago."

The deep, gurgling voice taunted, "The whelp needs lessons, I see. Yes, I am the Beither of long ago, and that is not all. I am the green Chinese Dragon King. I am Leviathan. I have taken many forms over the centuries and will do so for centuries to come."

Red realized, "You were the slimy beast in the sea as I stood on the ship's deck that day near the Pillars of Hercules. The sea dragon I battled and bested four hundred years ago."

The sea dragon smacked the water angrily with the tip of its tail. "You did not best me, mariner. You simply survived to battle another day. Too bad none of you will survive long enough to teach the new wizard." He looked at me, his massive black eyes staring into my very soul. The effect was chilling, but I could feel Bo's strength and confidence cultivating courage and self-assurance in me. He has seen this dragon before.

Bo finally spoke deep and menacingly from his perch, "To get to him, you'll first have to go through me." I could feel the emotion through our connection, and I was momentarily taken aback at the ferocity of his devotion to me.

"I will get to him, dragon. I will save his death for last, and it will be the most satisfying of all." A bubbling growl filled with the sound of hissing water went on for ten seconds until it continued. "I can smell his ancestor's blood in him. It runs strong, but even the descendant of the one who slayed my mate will not survive this battle. Your killing will be the most satisfying of my life, kin of the Dragonslayer."

The sea dragon's coils rippled on the water like the crowd at a baseball game doing the wave, up and down, around the circumference of its massive body. Bo saw the body movement as a sign of a pending attack and let out a preemptive roar that probably shattered windows and set off alarms in the building above. He leaped from the rusting pump station directly at the beast in the water, blasting it with a torrent of flame hot enough to send towering flumes of steam to the cavern roof. Draco Marinus shrieked as it was marginally hit by Bo's attack, fortunate that it was able to submerge most of its coiled body in time.

Launching himself off the rocky ground high above the lagoon, Bo took to the air, ready for a bold dive at the sea dragon. As he reached the zenith of his flight, Draco Marinus flipped its tail from under the water, catching Bo on the flank and sending him into a nearby light truss. The lights crashed into the water below in a shower of sparks and crackling electricity, cutting the available light in the cavern by more than half.

Undaunted, Bocephus recovered from the sideswipe and dove at his enemy, digging his claws into the sea dragon's midsection. With another gurgling screech, the sea dragon submerged, taking Bo underwater with it. I know my dog, and he isn't going to give up that easily. He'll hold on as long as possible, even underwater in the sea dragon's preferred fighting arena.

The water roiled as the fight ensued, with occasional intertwined glimpses of the red and green dragons rising above the surface. Claws, coils, wings, heads, and tails all twisted together into one impossible visage that would send any cryptozoologist into a frenzy.

I could feel Bo's rage but also his cunning and intelligence. He was not in any trouble and felt very capable of continuing this battle underwater for a while longer. He would need air eventually, but not yet.

"Be ready to help the dog," Red exclaimed as the turbulent water sprayed and splashed the cavern. "The next time they surface, look for a weak spot to attack the sea dragon." We all took up a position near the water's edge, ready to strike when the opportunity came.

At that moment, the water went still. The lagoon sloshed one final time, and the black water ceased its movement. The water may have settled, but our thoughts certainly did not. Fraught with anxiety, I stared at the unmoving underground body of water, pouring all my will into added strength for my dragon in this battle. The minutes ticked by with no sign of movement. We waited silently, each of us not speaking aloud the thoughts that were yelling inside our heads. We should have moved in sooner, I thought. We should have had Bo's back and been more active participants in the battle. We could have done it together, but instead, we were waiting for his body to float to the surface.

Without warning, a surge and splash so massive the black water rose to touch the cavern wall, soaking us above the knee and nearly knocking Red over before he recovered his footing. A mighty ear-splitting roar echoed off the jagged cavern walls, causing us to return our gaze to the water where one mighty ancient dragon had surfaced in the middle of the lagoon.

One dragon. My dragon.

CHAPTER TWENTY-SEVEN

A FRUSTRATED DRAGON

"Escaped," Bo said to all of us as he walked out of the water. "He got away under the water." I could hear the anger and frustration in his voice. His tail flicked and twitched like an angry cat's as he approached.

Bocephus was covered in bite marks from the sea dragon's massive teeth, and there were deep slices on his right leg from the sharp fins that ran the length of the sea dragon's body. Jim began an enchantment to hasten healing, and I could already see the wounds stitching themselves closed as his hands wavered over them.

"There's a tunnel that leads away from here, and I was too large to fit more than my head and neck."

An image formed in my mind of a French Bulldog swimming furiously through a narrow water-filled tunnel. I knew that thought was coming from Bo as he wondered if that would have been the best course of action.

"No," I said quickly. "Definitely not. That would have been much too dangerous."

My non-sequitur statement brought quizzical looks from my three elder compatriots, who waited patiently for me to explain. Their sideways-cocked heads and raised eyebrows were all the communication necessary.

"I can sometimes hear Bo's thoughts, and vice-versa. Our bond gets a little stronger every day. He thought he should have transformed into his smaller form to chase the sea dragon down the tunnel to the river if that's where it leads."

"That's a fine way to become a wee snack," John Patrick said with a chuckle. "You're going to have to fight a dragon as a dragon, not a pup."

Bo snuffed and turned away, exposing his other side for Jim's attention. The wounds on this side weren't as bad. I wondered how badly he had injured Draco Marinus in return.

"I got him good," Bo offered without my asking out loud. "He'll stay hidden for a while to recover."

"Thinking back to something the dragon said to me," I said, putting some puzzle pieces together. "What exactly did he mean when he called me kin of the Dragonslayer?"

"It's been apparent to me for quite some time that you are more than you realize and more than we expected you to be," Red said. "We suspected a powerful lineage even before you produced the amulet that belonged to the legendary dragonslayer of yore, but the sword clinched it for us. It once belonged to the legendary George the Dragonslayer. One of your ancestors was the greatest dragonslayer of all time, and his possessions have been passed down to you."

It seemed too unlikely. My grandpa's name was George, but he wasn't old enough to have lived that long ago. Considering how old the three Protectors standing before me are, maybe I'm wrong. Maybe magic made it possible. Did Grandpa George intentionally hide this knowledge from me to keep me from following in his footsteps? There could have been some other reason, but I couldn't come up with anything that made sense. My head was spinning enough that I took a seat on a rocky outcropping.

"I need to think about this for a minute."

Red still had more to say. "I also think your Grandpa George had been living here in town for a very long time, watching over the Protectors in case we ever were called into action and needed his help. Many years ago, one of our group members decided to leave this life behind. Perhaps he didn't go very far away to begin his new life and raise a family. It's easy for a wizard to change his appearance, and with skills like his, he could have easily kept himself concealed from us."

Wildly, it all made sense. My grandparents always supported me and my emerging powers, even while my parents didn't understand me. My mom and dad simply didn't know the things I was telling them were real, and my grandparents knew better regarding the true ways of the world.

"Aren't we an unlikely pair," Bo snuffed as he downsized to a dog and headed for the metal stairs.

He wasn't wrong. The grandson of a dragonslayer is now best friends with a dragon, not to mention the mental bond that was growing stronger by the day. The Protectors had never seen or heard of that part of the equation before, and they weren't quite sure what to make of it.

Chapter Twenty-Eight

A Fresh Start

I'm not your typical wizard from the movies or books. If you exclude the dragon in my apartment disguised as a dog, I live a fairly ordinary life. I go to work 6 days a week, flirt with the pretty girl at the sandwich shop downstairs, and when I need a haircut, I go to the barbershop across the street. I walk to the grocery store a few blocks away twice a week, even in the winter. A brisk walk in the cold keeps the blood pumping.

The only "magical" thing I do regularly at home is smudge my apartment every full moon. My grandma always taught me that burning sage helps to clear out the negative energy that accumulates, even if that's only from my own negative thoughts and doubts. There have been plenty of those since the confrontation with Draco Marinus. The smudging process always improves my mood, for whatever it's worth. Burning the sage is a respected, ancient spiritual ritual for the purification of a house or building.

I start in the bedroom, furthest from the front door, and light the white sage stick. Waving it around so the smoke wafts into every corner, I walk through the apartment, repeating, "I break up and release all negative and stagnant energy in this place." Through the kitchen and living room, then out the door and down the stairs, where the negative energy flows out the front door and into the street. I haven't talked to Valerie about it yet. I'm not sure what she'll say. I know she likes me, and she's not a judgmental person.

I do that every month on the night of the full moon, and that night is tonight. I need all the positive energy I can create. I have a big date with Valerie tomorrow.

CHAPTER TWENTY-NINE

DATE NIGHT

An uneventful week had passed since the battle in the cavern under the old factory, and I was as nervous as a cat at a dog pound, sitting across from the most gorgeous woman I had ever known in my life. Even though we saw each other multiple times every week, I always had an easy exit since she was working. This time, however, it was just the two of us. No distractions, no easy out when I got uncomfortable. I could feel the sweat running down my sides as I looked at Valerie. She made me feel so happy and skittish at the same time. Thankfully, she was never at a loss for words. That's a built-in part of her job, I suppose. Always able to make small-talk with the customers so they feel more at ease. I wasn't totally at ease without my sword nearby, but I didn't want to try and explain why I was suddenly carrying a walking stick like a frail old man or bourgeois rich kid.

"Mai Tai's and Crab Rangoon," Valerie said with a smile that filled the entire room. "My favorite! I can't wait to try their Kung Pao Chicken." Suddenly, she asked with alarm, "You aren't allergic to peanuts, are you?"

"Nothing to fear there," I assured her. "I'm not allergic to anything at all." Except for dating beautiful women, I thought. I seemed to be breaking out into hives or something. My whole face felt flushed every time she looked at me with those big brown eyes from across the table, and my hands were so sweaty I could barely pick up a glass.

"I am such an idiot," I said out loud. Crap.

"Wilder Blackwood, why would you say such a thing? What do you mean?" Valerie asked, putting her drink down and looking at me with such directness and caring that it made me sweat even more.

Shit. How do I cover such a dumb move?

"I uhhhh ... I'm such an idiot I didn't even ask you how your day was." Smooth, I thought.

"Just a normal day on Main Street," she replied. "It's Friday, so a lot of people stopped in after work to grab a couple of beers to wrap up the work week. I made a ton of sandwiches today. Everybody goes a little extra on payday!"

Valerie took a sip from her drink, ready with another story before she set the glass back down.

"Did you hear on the news about the missing man up in Baxter State Park? Everybody is talking about it. He was an experienced hiker and everything, and he's the second guy to disappear this week. The warden service says the two aren't connected, but people are starting to wonder."

"I hadn't heard. I've been kinda busy with other stuff. Where exactly did you say?"

At that moment, a woman sitting at the table in the front window screamed bloody murder and leaped back from her chair. The rest of their group jumped back a split second later, shouting with alarm at the scene on the street out front. An F-150 pick-up next to the curb went from a truck to a pancake in the blink of an eye. The SUV parked behind it abruptly flipped end-over-end into the middle of the road, and the fire hydrant twenty feet away popped off the sidewalk like someone flicking a dandelion off the stem.

"Shit," I said under my breath. "Shit shit shit, I know what that is."

Valerie stared at me. "An earthquake? I didn't feel anything," as she looked left and right around the room. People were running for the back emergency exit since the front door led to the sidewalk out front.

I knew the weird occurrences happening on the street weren't so odd after all if you knew an invisible sea dragon was making its way down the road. Smashing trucks, flipping cars, and popping fire hydrants were all part of a day's work for Draco Marinus. It was a dragon concealed from view by magic and wreaking havoc on the street outside, only a block away from the river. There could only be one reason it was making a public appearance slithering down a busy road: to get noticed by Bocephus and me. I noticed, alright, and now I had to do something about it. There's no way I'm tackling this without him by my side.

Thinking fast, I told Valerie, "We've got to get to Bo. He'll be scared if he hears all this commotion happening outside."

"Of course, let's hurry!" She quickly jumped to her feet and picked up her purse from the empty chair next to her without realizing my apartment wasn't within earshot of this restaurant. "We can come back to pay the check later."

Grabbing her hand, I led her out the back door to where everyone else was already heading. Nothing else could have caused that scene on the street besides a dragon. A dragon that nobody could see because of their natural cloaking spell. The street out front was like something from a movie. Multiple cars flipped over in the middle of the road, water shooting into the air from the broken hydrant, and people running around with no direction or sense of what to do. But I knew what I had to do. I needed to get home to my dragon.

We ran across the parking lot to my car and jumped in. I twisted the key, and the engine fired up before Valerie could click her seatbelt into place. Dodging the people still wandering the lot, we exited to a side street and navigated the short distance across the bridge back to Main Street. Since no parking spaces were available, I popped the passenger side over the curb and onto the sidewalk in the loading zone in front of Valerie's shop. "Wait for me here," I told her. "I'll get Bo and meet you in the store."

Even though she looked confused, Valerie nodded her head in agreement. "Hurry," she said. She leaned over, kissed me full on the lips, and looked directly into my eyes when she said, "Be careful."

Before the front door of the store came to a close, I heard Bo bark from upstairs. "It's about time you got home. We need to go!" His voice rang in my head.

He didn't even wait for me to get him. The window screen on my third-floor window tore open, and my little French bulldog plummeted toward the sidewalk below. Before his paws hit the cement, Bo transformed into his magnificent true form of Terra Draconis. The moment of change was stunning and majestic; his body swelled and expanded, and his wings appeared, extending from his back and unfurling in the evening air. His neck elongated as scales began to flash in the glow of the streetlight. Once short and stubby, his legs grew longer and thicker as sinew and muscle appeared by magic, the uncloaking and transformation of an almost impossible nature happening in midair. His coloring changed to all the reds in the spectrum, from the palest rose to rich crimson and even dark burgundy. The ground shook as he hit the sidewalk and pavement of the street, rattling windows and setting off nearby car alarms with the sheer force of his landing.

"Get on." Simple and direct. I leaped up as my heart began racing with the sudden adrenaline surge. I settled into my rider's position, my legs finding their familiar place as my hand grabbed the spikes that served as handlebars so I wouldn't fall off and die. With a deep exhale of breath, Bo leaped into the air, his powerful claws digging into the pavement, sending cracks spider-webbing across the street. The force was dizzying, not unlike what a jet fighter pilot feels upon takeoff. A scene from Top Gun inappropriately came to mind, "I feel the need, the need for speed," as the ground dropped away.

Our growing physical connection was unmistakable as I felt the energy surge through our connected bodies when Bo pushed off, and in the blink of an eye, we were high above the streetlights and rooftops of our little coastal town.

The cool evening air rushed against my face as we canvassed the city, the air filled with the scent of rain about to come. Below, the city lights spread in every direction, split by the inky ribbon of darkness that was the Saco River.

The wind rushed past my ears. I could feel Bo's heartbeat pounding against his flank, and I mentally tried to calm him. It was not an easy task since my heart was also racing, and every one of my senses were heightened in preparation of encountering Draco Marinus again.

With a few more powerful flaps of his wings, we soared over the river and into the next town, over the restaurant Valerie and I had sat in only a minute before. Valerie! What will she think happened to me? We crisscrossed the city, Bo scanning the environment with eyes better than mine, able to see light in spectrums I could only imagine.

We stayed in the air high above the city lights for hours as we searched, even after the rain had begun to fall. The droplets cut against my skin as we flew, like tiny needles pricking every exposed bit of me. Bo was moving at a speed I've rarely seen, quickly covering as much area as possible. I shielded my eyes with one hand while holding tightly with the other, wishing I had my goggles. Bo's fast turns and wild maneuvers never surprised me, though. I always knew they were happening a split second before they did. We covered the entire city from the air, then down the river, out to sea, and back again. There was no sign of the other dragon, the eternal nemesis of my Bocephus.

"I think he's just an asshole that likes to cause trouble," Bo said when I asked him what would motivate Draco Marinus to come out of the water and destroy a city street.

As the sun rose, we could see the trail of destruction caused by the dragon. It began at the river's edge, cut a clear path through connecting streets, and back to the river a few blocks away. Cars flipped, windows broken, and a few storefronts will have an argument with their insurance company in the morning. They'll blame it on high-velocity straight-line winds channeled between buildings down the city street that hit with a tornado-like force, and nobody will know how to argue differently. I can't imagine how bad it will be if this expands to a larger scale.

Now, I need to catch up with Valerie. I'll tell her that Bo was scared from all of the noise outside and ran off when I opened the door. That's a good reason for me to have disappeared all night without calling or texting her.

"Here be dragons to be slain, here be rich rewards
to gain; / If we perish in the seeking, why, how
small a thing is death!"
Dorothy L. Sayers, Catholic Tales and Christian
Songs

CHAPTER THIRTY

THE VIEW FROM ABOVE

I started bringing Bo to work. I couldn't risk getting an opportunity to go after the sea dragon and not having Bo near enough to be effective immediately. He spent my shifts wandering around the grounds of the old factory buildings, sniffing for snacks and lost cats. I didn't ask questions, and he didn't tell me any stories that disgusted me. That seemed fair enough.

On occasion, he'd transform and take flight over the city or across the river. Sometimes, he'd follow the river out to the sea, hoping to catch a glimpse of the other dragon. I never needed to worry about him, thanks to the strong bond we now had. We always knew exactly where each other was, our moods, and a general idea of our thoughts. It turns out dragons are very focused, and Bo's thoughts don't stray much from food and his search.

My thoughts, however, strayed constantly. So much so that Bo often complained that I was distracting him with the cacophony in my head about movies I'd seen, sandwiches I had recently eaten, and mainly about the girl I wanted to spend time with.

"Just take her back to your apartment," he said. "Nature will take its course."

"It doesn't work like that with people. Maybe that's what dragons do, but human women want a little more courtship and flirting."

"You're scared. More scared of her than you are of the other dragon."

Bo was right. I was as nervous as a long-tailed cat in a room full of rocking chairs whenever I was around Valerie. One look from her and my stomach flips like I just ratcheted up the hill on an enormous roller coaster and left my stomach three cars behind when it went down the massive drop.

"Dork."

Where does he learn this stuff?

"I'm almost done with my shift. Come pick me up," I mentally messaged Bo. I want to take a flight inland to take a look upriver.

Fifteen minutes later, we were in the air. I have learned to love the feeling of freedom and joy that comes from being a dragon rider. I'm the only one in hundreds of years, Bo told me. His wings barely made a noise as they beat against the air, propelling us forward and keeping us in the sky high above the buildings that dotted the riverbank. As we passed beyond the city limits and into a more rural area, the multi-colored shades of farmland dotted the ground below us. Flying over fields of corn and potatoes, barns and haybales filled out the idyllic scene. The patchwork quilt of crops is stitched together by dirt roads meant for tractors and other farm equipment, some of it moving across the ground, kicking up dust clouds in the dry air. The gently rolling land is like small waves in a calm sea, creating a tranquil effect. The late afternoon sun, golden hour, shines down on the two-lane roads and farm fields below, and the air smells fresh and earthy, even from up here.

Shaking me out of my reverie with an unexpected lurch, Bo swooped down toward a field of brown and white Hereford cows as they munched their way through the afternoon on the grass and clover.

"I want to know why you like hamburgers so much," he told me.

"You can't do that!" I yelled toward his ears. "That farmer will freak out if his cows go missing, especially if someone notices any strange activity as it happens. They won't see us, but it'll sure be an odd disappearance!"

"They'll just blame it on aliens," Bo suggested. "I can also burn a big circle into the field like the crop circles on that alien TV show we watched."

I wasn't sure if he was kidding or not, but I definitely didn't want Bo to snatch up a cow in his claws and fly off with it. We were only twenty feet above the ground when Bo let out a roar and dropped his invisibility spell. With a spray of fire ten feet over the cow's heads, they began to scatter in surprise, making a loud racket as all fifty or so started to moo all at once.

Vanishing from view once again and gaining altitude, Bo's deep, gravelly voice did something I had never heard before. He laughed. Loud and boisterously, like it was the funniest thing anyone had ever seen. A dragon laughing is not a normal sound. It was deep and guttural, rattling his ribcage and echoing through my head.

"Gotcha," he guffawed. "I enjoyed that. Jokes are good."

Bo's mighty wings pushed us higher into the sky, and the sun felt even more potent. There were no clouds in the sky, and our view of the countryside below was the same as if we were flying in a small private plane. It didn't scare me anymore. I knew I was safe.

CHAPTER THIRTY-ONE

BO'S BEACH DAY

The sun was just peeking over the horizon as we flew over the pier in Old Orchard Beach. These early morning jaunts had become a habit since summer arrived. The air was warm, even over the cooler Atlantic water below. The tourists weren't even awake yet, so we didn't have to be concerned about anyone noticing us, whether we were visible or not. Bo and I just flew, talked, and laughed, enjoying the freedom of clear minds and unfettered airspace.

The famous wooden pier juts out 500 feet into the Atlantic. The once-glorious tourist hotspot ends with a series of bars and restaurants sure to be crowded later today but sits still and silent in the early dawn hours. The view from above is much better than the view from the run-down pier. Tourists are usually surprised that a walk along the wide wooden structure mostly doesn't have a view of the beach and ocean. The desire to capitalize on the prime real estate has resulted in stalls of funky hot dogs, gimmicky games, and cheap souvenirs. There's only one spot along the entire length of the pier where you can see the water, but it's part of a nearby bar, so the view doesn't come for free.

We landed on the beach next to the pier. Bo's big dragon feet left massive prints in the wet sand. I'm sure some kids will see this later in the day and wonder who made the cool prints. They'll never even consider the possibility that a real-life dragon made the dragon footprints.

Nothing but the sound of the gently rolling surf and a few pre-dawn seagulls touched my ears. Bo the dragon became Bo the French Bulldog again, and we walked to our favorite breakfast spot nearby.

"Maybe we should come back down here for lunch this weekend. Valerie doesn't work on Sunday, and we can grab some pizza and pier fries and walk around for a while. There's always something interesting to see in the middle of tourist season, don't you think?"

Bo's answer was typical.

"A new season of my favorite show is coming out this weekend. I'll stay home while you two enjoy yourselves."

The Pine Tree Cafe was just a few blocks down the boulevard, just past the amusement park. It's been a family-run business since the 60s and always offers a friendly industry discount. I usually leave an extra-large tip for the server to make up the difference. We need to support each other, especially since tourists are notoriously stingy with tips. I sat at the counter to order while Bo wandered around outside for a while. He's not exactly a normal dog, so I didn't have to worry about him wandering off.

"Welcome back, Wilder. It's been a few weeks since you've been in for breakfast!"

Babette has been here since before I was born. She remembers my parents coming here for breakfast and my grandparents before that. Her parents came from Quebec and opened the place in 1963. Babette was born shortly thereafter. Working at the diner is the only job she's ever known. Even though she was born in Old Orchard Beach, her French-Canadian heritage was boldly apparent in her accent.

"Thanks for noticing. I've been a little preoccupied. It's been a busy past few months."

"Hopefully, with that young lady you keep talking about," she said with a wink. "Making any progress there?"

"We had our first date a few days ago. It was memorable, that's for sure."

Babette stopped refilling the napkin dispenser and gave me a look that could have stopped a dragon's rampage.

"You be a gentleman, monsieur. That's the only way to catch a pretty mademoiselle."

I sat my Welcome To Maine coffee cup down with a clank and laughed at her assumption of what my comment meant.

"Je suis toujours un bon garçon," practicing my French and assuring her I'm always on my best behavior.

Babbette laughed and clapped her hands as she slipped my regular breakfast in front of me without waiting for my order. When I looked up, the line cook nodded through the kitchen pass, acknowledging that he had also seen me arrive and fixed it for me.

"I look forward to the day you bring her in for breakfast so I can meet her myself."

Dipping into the runny egg yolk with the first bite of toast, I agreed with her.

"From your lips to God's ears, my grandma always said that."

Fifteen minutes of casual conversation later, I paid the check and headed out the door. Mentally calling for Bo, he came trotting down the street to rejoin me. The sun was a bit higher in the sky, and the day was warming up nicely. People started appearing on the street, beginning their day in Vacationland.

As we walked back toward the main square, tourists crossed our path on their way from their motels to the beach, folding chairs and towels in hand to stake out a spot in the sun and clean white sand. Old Orchard Beach is a popular destination and has been for well over a hundred years. Most of the signs on local shops and restaurants are written in English and French, making the holiday more welcoming for the Quebecois families, making up more than 60 percent of the summer tourists.

We were on the sidewalk that ran alongside the amusement park, just past the rollercoaster, when the screams started. The sounds of distress weren't coming from the people on the rides because they were still an hour from opening for the day. These screams were coming from the beach on the other side of the narrow amusement park that ran between the main road and the sand, and they weren't letting up.

"Bo, we need to get over there fast. That could be you-know-who in the ocean!"

Within ten seconds, I was on the back of my massive red dragon as he leaped into the air. Bo's powerful haunches flexed and propelled us up and over the fence, and one flap of his wings carried us above the pirate ship ride and log flume. As we passed over the bumper cars, the beach and ocean popped into view. The sandy expanse stretched left and right as far as my eyes could see, gleaming in the early morning sun across the water to the east.

We may have left behind a tourist or two who wondered where the man and his dog suddenly disappeared, but there was no time to be more discreet. This could be a dangerous encounter, potentially life-threatening to anyone on the beach already.

"I don't see anything, do you?"

Bo's dragon sight enabled him to see in more spectrums than my poor old human vision, but there was still nothing to be seen. The screams picked up in intensity again.

"To the left, on the other side of the pier! Get up higher so we can see what's happening on the other side," I urged.

Three seconds later, we were above the pier with a clear view of the other side. Our vision was partially blocked by the two-story bar on the front side of the structure. Now that we were on the other side, we could see what was causing all the excitement.

Teenagers.

Three boys on ATVs were doing donuts in the wet sand left behind after the tide went out an hour ago. They were surrounded by twenty or thirty other kids, all screaming in encouragement as they spun circles in the sand. The beach patrol was on the way, two of their side-by-sides rounding the corner from the front of the pier. The crowd scattered, and the three hooligans took off down the beach, quickly shrinking smaller and smaller. Thankfully, it was early, so only a few people were on the beach: dog walkers, joggers, and people saving a good spot for later.

The cops were savvy enough to see the inherent danger in a chase, so they let off the throttle and frustratingly watched the boys head out of sight. These things happen a few times every summer, but usually nobody gets hurt. The town will bring the beach grooming machine back to rake out the ruts and grooves, and within an hour, nobody will even know this happened.

"That's a huge relief, but a good lesson never to let our guard down."

Gaining altitude again over the shoreline, Bo responded with a grunt as we turned back toward home.

"I want this to end. The chance for many deaths is much too great."

CHAPTER THIRTY-TWO

THE CALLING

It's been three weeks with no sign of Draco Marinus. Red, Jim, and John Patrick believe it's still nearby because the dragon's sole purpose now is to regain the treasure they hid long, long ago. I've never even seen the treasure. Jim told me the chests are in an almost inaccessible place to keep them safe from accidental discovery.

I have my sword and Grandpa's Amulet of Illumination, and both are powerful objects of magic. Jim had the clever idea of changing my sword's concealment spell to make it more modern and useful. I don't need a cane or walking stick; a martial arts bo came to mind, but that would look equally odd.

A man can't walk around town carrying a 6-foot staff without drawing attention. An umbrella is not under consideration, even though that's Red's way of concealing his sword. It works for him, but not for me.

This morning, while putting on my pants, I thought, "Red, can I hide the sword as anything at all, or does it need to be an inflexible object?"

"I don't follow. Give me an example. Do you want it to look like you're carrying around an iPad or something? It needs to be similar in length to the sword. The concealment spell isn't the same as your dragon changing size. I have no idea how he does that bit of magic."

"How about a leather belt," I offered for his consideration. "I thought of it this morning when I was getting dressed. A belt is of similar width and length."

John Patrick stepped over to join our conversation, "Aye, lads. That will work pure dead brilliant. I once knew a wizard who concealed his sword in his wife's long hair. 'Twas only a wig, and she was as bald as a cucumber!"

With a laugh around the room, we set to removing the spell on the sword and replacing it with the new concealment. Once I wrapped the belt around my waist, I felt more assured and confident that my grandfather's sword would never be far from my hand.

"I just hope your pants never fall down in a fight!" John Patrick needled, and we all laughed again, even Bo.

In my off time, the men have been teaching me the history of our order and helping me refine and develop my magic. Of course, they've never experienced having a dragon for a buddy, so that part is a mystery to them.

"Seven Protectors came to the new world with the leather-wrapped chests of dragon treasure," Red shared with me. "Three came here, John Patrick, Jim, and your grandfather, to hide the chests they brought with them. I joined them later when I returned from the Mediterranean on a scouting mission."

"But what became of the others?" I wanted to know.

"We thought it best to split the treasure into two separate hiding places, and that group did not know where the other had gone. That way, no man or dragon could discover the information and reunite the treasure."

"So you don't know where the three other chests went? Can't you track them somehow?"

"That would defeat the purpose of splitting them up. They are lost to time."

John Patrick jumped in, "But that slimy beastie knows this treasure is here somewhere and will never stop until the chests are in its possession."

He was right. The only thing stopping it right now is Bo's presence, but Draco Marinus won't be stymied for long.

Without warning, Bo let out a bark. "It's time," he said. "He is calling out to me. He is challenging me. We need to get to the river."

He was panting at the door down the stairs before I could grab my shoes. The others would catch up in Red's truck.

"My armour is like tenfold shields, my teeth are swords, my claws spears, the shock of my tail is a thunderbolt, my wings a hurricane, and my breath death!"

Smaug

<h1>Chapter Thirty-Three</h1>

<h1>THE BATTLE ON THE RIVERFRONT</h1>

Draco Marinus was waiting when we flew within sight of the river. His head was lifted above the water on a wavering, sinewy neck, watching the sky for any sign of Bo's approach. From that vantage point, the sea dragon could see for a half mile in any direction except for one. The old four-story brick factory building with its massive two-hundred-dred-fifty-foot-tall smokestack blocked the view of our arrival from the south. I'd like to say it was a purposeful tactic, but it was pure accident.

Neither dragon had much time to prepare or react. By the time they saw each other, they were almost within striking distance.

"Hold on for the ride of your life!" Bo warned me as he plummeted from the sky in a power dive, ready to attack. His massive wings flexed and pumped, increasing our velocity.

Releasing a mighty torrent of superheated magical flame at Draco Marinus, we pulled back up at the last moment, avoiding impact with the water and the other dragon. When we cleared the cloud of steam caused by the heat, I looked back to see that it was a miss and a frightening one at that. Holding on tightly, we rocketed skyward and attacked again, keeping the sea dragon on the defensive in the middle of the river.

Bo's clawed feet clutched out as we reached the terminus of the dive, grabbing for a hold on the dragon below. Squirming from his reach, the sea dragon lashed upward with his tail, encircling Bo's feet in a hold worthy of an enormous, hungry python. It had been a trap. He was waiting for Bo to come close enough that he could get a tight hold. The slimy green bastard misjudged Bo's strength and instead was lifted from the river, shaking and blasting fire toward us above. It had no proper aim and instead shot randomly across the nearby area like a fire hose out of control. The jets of flame blew a dozen cars in the nearby parking lot to bits and tires on other vehicles exploded from the heat. The shrill car alarms filled the air, blending with the shouts and screams of bystanders.

Recognizing the grave danger to people nearby, Bo released the dragon to flop back into the water, where it dove beneath the surface to regroup. That's when the screaming started.

"Bo, everyone can see us and the other dragon!"

In the throes of their bombastic battle, the two dragons had sacrificed their cloaking spells for more power, funneling every ounce of energy into the defeat of the other. That meant every single person in sight was now watching two colossal dragons in a monumental fight above the river in their little Maine town.

People screamed and ran from the riverbank walkway while others ran toward the scene. Those morons all held their phones high in their hands, recording the moment for posterity. That was something we couldn't allow. Jim, Red, and John Patrick had arrived moments before and formed a triangle in the parking lot, each with his back to the center and facing outwards. Hands raised and palms thrust outward, a blue and yellow orb radiated from them as fast-moving as an explosion.

The result was the malfunction of every electronic device within five miles. Every car alarm was suddenly silenced all at once. The blast radius of their electromagnetic wave pulse was so powerful that every item affected would never work again. There would also never be a recording of this battle to live forever on the internet.

We needed to combine our powers to help Bo, but I couldn't do that while I was riding on his back. He picked up my mental signal and landed ever so briefly on the pavement, giving me seconds to jump off before launching himself back into the air. There was a massive bloody clawed footprint on the parking lot, which meant Bo was wounded.

"It's just a flesh wound," he mentally shouted back. "Don't distract me."

Running over to the Protectors, I found them gathered around Jim, who was lying on the ground next to a big black SUV with flattened, melted tires. He had collapsed after their EMP attack, and the others dragged him here for cover.

"What happened? Is he okay?"

"He just needs a few minutes to recover," Red replied. "That took a lot of energy for all of us."

"We may not have a few minutes," I said as I looked at the river, searching for any sign of the lurking leviathan.

The sea dragon's head burst from beneath the water's surface at a fantastic speed, rocketing upward until the beast's entire body was above the surface. It was longer than I expected it to be, easily as long as five connected train cars and almost as big in circumference.

Bocephus, the Terra Draconis, jerked sideways in midair. I could feel his anger but also his calmness and purity of thought. He wasn't letting emotions get the best of him or letting his feelings affect his actions. A few pumps of his massive red wings took him high above the ground as he perched on top of the two-hundred-fifty-foot-tall brick smokestack on the factory. It was at least forty feet wide at the base, unquestionably strong enough to hold him at the top. We'd soon find out. Added to the stature of the building above the riverbank and granite retaining wall, he was now almost four hundred feet above the river, out of reach from the sea dragon.

Then, even more of the unexpected happened. The sea dragon took flight, sprouting a triple set of wings along its long body. The wings were vast and leathery, similar to Bo's, but in shades of translucent green, more like oceanic hues. They flapped in unison, carrying the sea dragon toward Bo on the brick smokestack. The dragon flew in an s-pattern, undulating through the air the same way it swam through the water. In the air, it was even more incongruous to the world around us. Beneath its tail, a trail of mist and water droplets fell, creating a fog effect around the dragon as it moved toward Bo and the smokestack.

Draco Marinus opened its mouth, exposing rows of shark-like teeth, sharp, jagged, and deadly. The creature's green scales flickered iridescently in the sunlight as it continued the undulating flight, landing on the brick smokestack fifty feet below where Bo's claws clenched the rim.

Bo spread his wings wide and twisted his neck downward, roaring to the dragon below and belching a flame that melted the shingles on the building roof hundreds of feet below. With an ear-splitting screech as a response, Draco Marinus twisted its body around the enormous circular chimney that had stood over the city and river bank since the beginning of the twentieth century and began to squeeze. The powerful muscles along its body undulated once, and the tower crumbled like an angry child kicking over a tower of Legos.

Bricks tumbled onto the roof of the building, and even more bricks were pushed from the top as Bo attempted to gain leverage and take flight as his mighty wings beat against the air high above the ground. As the smokestack fell, the sea dragon also dropped away. The unlikely flying creature dove for the river, its descent controlled by the three sets of immense wings that seemed to fold back within the body as it reached the water. Then it was gone. There was nothing left but the destruction and the terrified people who witnessed the battle above the river.

Mentally, I shouted to my dragon, "Bo, you need to hide yourself! We'll make everyone forget they saw any of this."

"He's gone back to the cavern. I will find him," and he vanished from sight.

Jim was now sitting up, which was perfect because we needed his help and expertise. We needed a spell or incantation to make everyone who saw a dragon battle forget it ever happened. We don't need to fill in the memory gap or explain the smashed cars and busted phones, and we only need them not to remember dragons were battling over the Saco River.

Red knew the answer, "That's a Blankstrike spell. It causes a sudden, irreversible memory wipe to anyone within a certain distance. We used it in Italy during World War 1 for the same reason."

"There were dragons in Italy during the First World War?" I asked.

"See, laddie, it works!" John Patrick said with a chuckle.

Grasping each other's hands to increase the flow of magical energies, John Patrick said quietly, "Memoria fugat, umbra recedit, Quod vidisti, nunquam retinet."

The moment he finished the incantation, Red and Jim repeated the spell together. The effect was instantaneous. The parking lot was now filled with people wandering about, wondering what had happened to their cars.

"Was there an explosion?" one woman asked.

"Those damn kids and their fireworks," an old man shouted to his wife. "They're nothing but trouble these days."

"I think it was an earthquake, but I didn't feel it!" a man walking his dog remarked.

"Oh my God, what happened across the river to the factory? Look at the smokestack!"

An earthquake would be the simplest explanation for people to accept. With the fires, burnt-out cars, and collapsed old smokestack on the factory, anything plausible would be accepted by the townspeople who didn't remember anything about dragons.

It looks like the guys have another little spell they need to cast. I need to run after Bo before something awful happens. This isn't a battle he should fight alone.

"Dragons are not merely beasts to be slain; they
are challenges to be overcome."

Christopher Paolini, Eragon

CHAPTER THIRTY-FOUR

WITH GREAT POWER

By the time I navigated my way to the cavern entrance and descended the clanky ancient grated metal stairs, Bo was already at the water's edge. His legs were poised and ready for an assault, the scales on his body reflecting the lights above like a red prism. The twisted and broken light trusses hung from the cavern ceiling, only providing half of the light they were built for. Some of the lights still worked, so we weren't in complete darkness. For the moment, I didn't need my amulet to be able to see. I whipped off my belt with a leathery snap, and it instantly lengthened and transformed into my grandfather's powerful legendary sword. Weapon in hand, I took up a position next to Bo. His attitude made me feel stronger, both magically and with strength of will and determination. The fact that I was next to an enormous, mighty, fire-breathing dragon didn't hurt my self-confidence, either.

"How did you get back down here?" I quizzed. "A dragon doesn't fit through the door, and a dog can't turn a doorknob."

"Guard let me in. He was easy to convince," came the response. No further details, so I didn't press. His eyes never came off the water.

Bo scanned the surface of the black underground lagoon, watching through all spectrums of light to catch any warning of movement. He held his head high, panning back and forth for a better view, not wanting to miss the slightest hint of movement. The silence overtook the cavern for what seemed like an hour but was probably only ten minutes. An occasional drop of moisture from the ceiling made me flinch, even though I tried to remain still.

"You need to calm down," Bo said as he spread his wings in a dragon mimic of stretching one's arms. "Your jumpiness is unnerving."

"I'm so sorry!" I whispered back. "I've never battled a giant sea dragon before, and it makes me a little anxious."

That was an understatement. I have learned so much in the last few months, but this is a big leap in expectation for my growing power. The others have so much more experience, but considering their age, I'm not sure how much they are physically capable of. Do centuries-old men have the stamina to fight against an ancient enemy? One thing they aren't lacking is confidence, though. I need to take a page out of their wizard playbook and believe more in yours truly. Doubting myself will only hinder my ability to get the job done.

The quiet clank of multiple pairs of shoes on metal stair grates alerted me to the Protector's presence. Red, Jim, and John Patrick had arrived on the catwalk above the cavern and begun walking down to the bottom. Drawing their swords, they spread out wordlessly and took positions around the lagoon. We were here, and we were ready.

It only took seconds for something to happen, almost as if Draco Marinus was waiting for us all to be assembled in the cavern before he surfaced.

"He is rising," Bo said quietly. "The arrogant slimeball has been lying on the bottom of the lagoon, waiting for us to all be together. He will not defeat us. He will not reclaim his treasure."

Draco Marinus rose up in the water, dead center in the middle of the dark waters of the lagoon. At first, we could only see the top of his head and his eyes. Two horn-like spikes on top dripped water as he continued to rise slowly. His face appeared arrogant and sneering, if that's even possible for a dragon. His neck was long and glistening in the dim lighting, and the green scales gave off an ominous glow. He was dangerous looking, but Bo was every bit as fierce and deadly.

With a shout of "Alba gu bràth," John Patrick began to glow with ancient power, drawing from the ley lines deep beneath the bedrock of the cavern. Jim and Red also drew from that Earth power, becoming more powerful as they did. Maine is a rich and overlooked location for ley lines, from the coastal areas to Mount Katahdin to Acadia National Park and The Allagash Wilderness. It's the reason the Protectors chose this place.

It may be cliche, but the bad guys always like to boast. The sea dragon habitually taunts his opponents and talks too much.

"What a nice little sword you have there," he directed at John Patrick. "Do you think you can harm me with that little pricker? I'll barely feel it. And you," looking at Red. "I have destroyed ships at sea with barely more than a thought and thrash of my tail. What hope do you have of harming me?"

As Draco Marinus turned and opened his mouth to say something threatening to me, Bocephus released a tightly focused white-hot jet of fire directly into his mouth. This unexpected onslaught caused the sea dragon to rear back in pain, even letting out a roar of anger at receiving the first strike.

"He gets hurt on the inside," Bo let me know mentally. "Scales are his armor, but inside he is soft."

"Too bad he can't keep his mouth shut!" I replied sarcastically. "I could keep taunting him until he opens his mouth again to respond, and you can do it again."

"It will only work once," I hear Bo think. To all of us, he said, "It's time to attack. I will draw him closer to the water's edge to bring him within your reach."

Bo drew back, taking two steps in reverse. His opponent in the water perceived this as a retreat, emboldening the sea dragon to come closer and begin his offensive. Wordlessly this time, he reached the stone floor and stretched the top portion of his body toward Bo, who had backed toward the cavern wall.

"You are afraid," the sea dragon finally spoke in his dank and slithering tone. "You are afraid, and now you have nowhere to go. You must fight or die. Then I will seize the treasure and dominate this world as I dominated the sea for centuries before these foul creatures banished us from this realm."

He pulled his head up and back in a cobra-like striking position, not taking his eyes off Bo, creating the perfect moment for Red and Jim to attack from both sides. Sword in hand, each leaped toward the dragon, thrusting their blades directly between the scales where they could do the most damage. The scales would block an ordinary blow, but this was much more direct and effective.

In the split-second it took for Draco Marinus to react and whirl his head toward one side, both men had retreated well out of reach. Now it was Bo's turn, lunging forward with his mouth open, teeth like massive razor blades, snapping at the dragon's neck. Bo got in a good chomp and held tightly, forcing the sea dragon to turn his head away from the advancing men. All four of us were there now, driving our blades into the dragon between the scales, the only way to cause any injury. He lashed out with the only thing we couldn't control: his tail.

Flipping from beneath the water, the sea dragon's tail snapped toward us like a whip. It cracked past me, narrowly missing me and swiping across the blade of my sword. My grip was good, and I held tightly to the hilt, ready for another attack.

The dragon's body continued to thrash violently as Bo held his neck tightly, pinning the enemy to the cavern floor. Bo was larger and stronger, using one of his clawed feet to help pin the dragon down. The tail whipped around again, this time catching Jim from behind.

Jim was flung from his position next to the sea dragon and swept across the floor, sword clattering to the floor. His body landed with a wet, crunching sound against the cavern wall, where he lay unmoving.

My shock immediately turned into controlled anger. Channeling that energy, I jumped high as the tail thrashed toward me. As the iridescent scales and fins on the tail passed below me, I clearly envisioned my next move. The moment my feet hit the ground, I pushed all of my magic forward into Grandpa's sword. I sliced down on the dragon's tail, the sword cleanly hacking through it all the way to the stone floor. Draco Marinus let out a roar that would shake a building off its foundation. The detached ten-foot section of tail jerked a few times before laying still, no longer a threat.

"Back off," Bo warned us, and we listened. I don't know what he's planning, but he has a lot more experience with dragons than we do. We retreated twenty feet before Bo released the sea dragon.

"No!" Red exclaimed. "What are you ..."

Before our eyes, Bo transformed. The sea dragon no longer faced a mighty red nemesis who was already besting him in battle. Standing before him now was a small French bulldog, looking up defiantly. Draco Marinus reared back, looked down, and reacted instantly.

He ate him.

The dragon simply opened his mouth and scooped up my dog. Then, before I could even react and try to save Bo, the sea dragon simply ... exploded. Bits of gore and scales and flesh flew everywhere, covering us and the cavern walls with offal. There wasn't even a sound to accompany the fleshy explosion. Opening my eyes after wiping my face, I saw the one thing I did not expect to see. The dragon Bocephus was standing right in front of me, messy but unharmed.

"What ... how ... I don't understand!" I was at a loss for words.

Red knew right away, "He did it on purpose. He blew it up from the inside. It's like the story of the Ichneumon mythical mongoose who kills dragons by entering their mouth and killing them from the inside out."

I remembered when Bo flamed into the sea dragon's mouth and commented about hurting him from the inside. He made this plan back then!

"You knew," I shouted at him, partly happy and partly angry. "You knew you were going to do this! You could have been killed."

"I didn't have time to explain," Bo responded. "I wasn't sure it would work, but I had to try. With great power comes great responsibility."

"That's from Spiderman, and if he had chomped you instead of swallowing you whole, you would have never seen another movie. That slimy green bastard didn't even take a moment to think when he saw a chance to eat you."

Surrounded by our success in bloody little bits all around the cavern, John Patrick reminded us of one cost to this battle.

"Jim."

CHAPTER THIRTY-FIVE

SAYING GOODBYE

Since I didn't own a car, we had to borrow one from Parker. I felt bad lying to my boss, but I couldn't tell him the truth.

"Hey, your dad is an ancient wizard, and he never told you. Can I borrow your Explorer?"

Maybe someday, but not yet. I explained that Red needs me to run some errands for him and he was bringing John Patrick and Jim along, that was why he wouldn't want to come along for the ride. He was agreeable to the car loan and was working at the restaurant anyway. Parker may give me an odd look every now and then, but he doesn't ask any questions.

Technically, Jim was with us. He just wasn't alive anymore. It's been a long time since a Protector has died, let alone be killed in battle. We wrapped his body carefully in blankets, our movements slow and deliberate, as though the act of wrapping him was also to preserve the dignity of the man who had given his life to save the world. After loading Jim into the Ford, we drove to a secluded rocky shoreline. That's not too hard to find in Maine. Bo was with us and would be an integral part of the funeral ceremony. Traditionally, Protectors would be burned in a funeral pyre. That would tend to bring too much attention, but I came up with a similar and even more appropriate solution for our dearly departed friend.

Standing on the rocky shoreline in the afternoon glow everyone calls "the golden hour," I was reminded why I love life in Maine so much. The air felt thick with the scent of the briny water, mixing with the tang from the nearby pine trees that surrounded us. The sun flashed across the tips of each wave, and the wind blew in gently from the Atlantic, tugging at our clothing and tousling my hair. The ancient voice of the sea was loud and insistent as the rhythmic waves crashed on the rocks around us.

This part of the coastline is rugged, unlike the serene sandy beaches nearby. The weather-beaten granite boulders piled up along the shoreline protect the land beyond from the fury of the waves. Seaweed and moss cling to spots on the rocks, and tidal pools brimming with life dot the landscape to the left and right, the cold ocean water trapped within warmed in the day's sunshine.

The coastline curves gently to the left and right in this small, protected cove. Far offshore, a few fishing boats move silently on their way back from their day at sea, the sound of their engines shushed by the constant murmur of the waves. Seagulls spiral in the air overhead, their sharp calls cutting through the unrelenting quiet roar of the ocean.

Once we found the proper spot, out of sight of any other potential witnesses, we laid Jim's body out on the rocky shoreline. As we bowed our heads, John Patrick spoke a few words to honor him, reading the words of the Scottish poet Robert Burns.

"An honest man here lies at rest,
As e'er God with His image blest:
The friend of man, the friend of truth;
The friend of age, and guide of youth:
Few hearts like his, with virtue warm'd,

Few heads with knowledge so inform'd:

If there's another world, he lives in bliss;

If there is none, he made the best of this."

When he finished speaking, we raised our heads, and Bocephus took over the next and final part of the ceremony. Transforming to his mighty dragon form in a flash, Bo turned toward the earthly remains of our friend. With a slow and controlled fiery blast, the once-great Protector was gone in less than a minute. The unyielding streak of flame was blinding, a white-hot mix with flickers of gold, red, and orange. The air around the body crackled with energy as if the atmosphere around it was also being consumed. I wasn't entirely confident that the flare of light was solely from the flames. Jim's body seemed to be exuding its own glow as the fire consumed it. When it was over, only his ashes remained. They continued to emit faint twinkling points of light in the fading glow of the sunset until the last faded from view.

We all stood silently as a breeze picked up along the shoreline, as it often does, carrying Jim's ashes into the air and out to sea. It was a fitting end to a great life, protecting many lives who were unaware of his existence.

"We will gather together another day, my old friend," Red spoke to the wind as we turned away.

Chapter Thirty-Six

THE FINAL DECISION

Upstairs in their lookout tower room above the restaurant, Red and John Patrick had been speaking to each other in whispers for an hour. From the other side of the room, Bo and I pretended not to hear them, even though we plainly knew what they were talking about.

"Hey, guys," I spoke up. "This might be more productive if we all talked it over. This room is only twenty feet across, so Bo and I aren't having much trouble hearing you."

"Well ... I'm not sure how to address the problem with ... the problem in the room," Red replied reluctantly.

"Not long ago, I was the solution, not a problem," Bo snorted, little tendrils of smoke rising from his wet dog nostrils. "Now that the other dragon is gone, you are concerned about m e."

It is best to have it out in the open for discussion. Beating around the bush wouldn't get us anywhere, and there's no need to postpone the conversation any longer. We defeated the sea dragon and had Jim's funeral two weeks ago.

"You guys are worried that now there's no other dragon, Bo will blast us all and take back the dragon treasure for himself. Even though he doesn't know where the treasure is, and he has given no sign at all that he wants to find it. Am I right?

John Patrick looked at Bo, then at me. "A nod's as guid as a wink tae a blind horse. It's what dragons do, isn't it?"

"Let me explain," I continued.

"Aye, that's what I just asked ya to do. Can ye explain whit yer on aboot?"

"Bo's been with me for months, and he's never once mentioned the treasure. In fact, before you told him about it, he didn't even know it was here. He just knew he was drawn here for some mysterious reason. That reason was likely because of Draco Marinus. It's only logical for Terra Draconis to be pulled to the same location."

Bo had grown weary of listening to this exchange and said, "I don't care about the treasure. If there are no other dragons, there's no reason to keep and guard it. I don't feel the drive to seek it out."

"He's my dog," I said. "It's my choice. I choose for him to stay. There's nothing more to talk about.

Red tisked at me," He's more than a dog, son. He's a powerful elemental dragon. One this world hasn't seen in centuries." He stood up from the table and walked across the plank floor, boots tapping slowly until he reached the window. Red stood there and stared out at the river for a minute, thinking carefully.

Bo didn't give him the chance to go on, "I'm here, and I will help you. The treasure will stay hidden. I have no need. This is my new home. I like the snacks."

I wasn't sure if Bo meant the Twinkies or the cats or maybe a little bit of both. All eyes in the room were on me. I've only been in this wizard business for a few months, but the men who have served in their roles for hundreds of years wanted to hear what I had to say.

"We're down a man, a great one at that. This world is a more dangerous and frightening place than ever in history. We need help if we're going to continue the special role we play. Who better to help us than a freaking dragon."

I pointed at Bocephus. "That is a dragon sitting there. Have you ever in all of your years thought that something so amazing and powerful would be an ally? I can't think of any better team that could possibly exist. Wizards and a dragon, working together to keep the world safe from other magical, mysterious, and mystical forces."

I knew in my heart these words were valid. The stronger I become, the more I can feel the forces at work out there in the world. Even here in Maine, there are strange and mysterious places that are becoming more active.

"Have you seen the mysterious hiker disappearances near Mt. Katahdin in Baxter State Park? It's up to five people already this summer, and they're worried it might be a serial killer. The news said they've all vanished during thunderstorms."

Red looked up at me, startled, "The Thunderbirds have returned."

The Katahdin Wilderness is a very remote part of the state at the Northern tip of the Appalachian Trail, with over two hundred thousand acres of remote wilderness and forty mountain peaks. The area is undeveloped, with only dirt roads to access anywhere. While popular with hikers, the wilderness offers some of the most challenging conditions on the East Coast.

"There's powerful magic on that mountain, the Passamaquoddy and Penobscot Indians knew," Red acknowledged. "And no easy way to explore the area."

"Unless you've got a dragon."

John Patrick looked at Red. Standing tall and hiking up his pants, he said, "It looks like retirement is still a few years away, lads. I'll get my Bean boots. Wilder Blackwood, it's good to have you as a Protector!"

"The greatest adventure is what lies ahead."

J. R. R. Tolkien

ABOUT THE AUTHOR

Jon Shannon and his wife Lori have been married since 1995 and have two adult sons. They live in Saco, Maine.

A lifelong science fiction and urban fantasy fan, Jon has also been a cryptid enthusiast and mythologist since childhood.

Jon is a Maine Broadcasting Hall of Fame inductee and was named one of the Top 30 Country Program Directors in America by Radio Ink Magazine. For over 20 years, Jon has been a morning show host on the top country radio station in the state of Maine. Tune in to 101.9 WPOR any weekday morning for the fun with Jon, Joe and Courtney.

Jon's first book, "The Longest Summer," was a love story chosen by Amazon as the national #2 Hot New Release upon publication.

ACKNOWLEDGEMENTS

To my wife, Lori, thank you for your love, patience, and understanding during the long hours spent writing. I have a sneaky suspicion that you are delighted to have me out of your hair for hours at a time through the afternoons and late into the evenings so I won't complain about watching Bravo and The Food Network.

I write because I have tales to tell. I can't thank you, the reader, enough for following along and reading my stories. There is no point in writing if nobody is reading, so you have made a dream come true for me. While writing a completely different book, I had the idea for this book, and I couldn't get the story out of my head. I shelved the original project in favor of this one, which turned out to be a multi-book storyline. Sometimes, a story takes on a life of its own, and I felt compelled to let this one grow into whatever it was destined to be.

I've always been fascinated by my state's local history, mythology, and legends, so it's natural that it became a part of the story and will be even more significant in the future. Thank you for allowing me to exercise my imagination. I sincerely appreciate every moment you have given to me.

ALSO BY JON SHANNON

The Longest Summer